"Erin, I'm going

She said nothing.

"You don't think we're going to make it. Do you?"

"I've lost count of the times I thought we were both going to die. Whatever that thing is in that case you are hiding beside the bed, people are willing to kill for it."

"You still want me to leave it behind?"

He held his breath, waiting.

"No. My party died because of that thing, whatever it is. I've decided to see this through."

"For a minute I thought you were only willing to jump off trestle bridges after stray dogs."

"Jet isn't a stray. Her owners were murdered, just like my party." She lifted up on an elbow and stared down at him. Her hair fell across her face, shielding her expression. She stroked his forehead with a thumb.

"I just want you to stay with me. You know?"

"Planning on it." He cradled her jaw in his hand, and she turned to press a kiss against his palm.

ADIRONDACK ATTACK

JENNA KERNAN

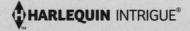

This story is dedicated, with love and admiration, to my mother, Margaret C. Hathaway, who drove me to school, swim lessons, summer camp, dance lessons, art lessons, the Adirondack Mountains and the American West. Who could have imagined the world was so big?

ISBN-13: 978-1-335-60454-5

Adirondack Attack

Copyright © 2019 by Jeannette H. Monaco

Recycling programs for this product may not exist in your area.

Printed in U.S.A.

www.Harlequin.com

Jenna Kernan has penned over two dozen novels and received two RITA® Award nominations. Jenna is every bit as adventurous as her heroines. Her hobbies include recreational gold prospecting, scuba diving and gem hunting. Jenna grew up in the Catskills and currently lives in the Hudson Valley in New York State with her husband. Follow Jenna on Twitter, @jennakernan, on Facebook or at jennakernan.com.

Books by Jenna Kernan

Harlequin Intrigue

Protectors at Heart

Survival Instinct
Adirondack Attack

Apache Protectors: Wolf Den

Surrogate Escape
Tribal Blood
Undercover Scout
Black Rock Guardian

Apache Protectors: Tribal Thunder

Turquoise Guardian
Eagle Warrior
Firewolf
The Warrior's Way

Apache Protectors

Shadow Wolf
Hunter Moon
Tribal Law
Native Born

Harlequin Historical

Gold Rush Groom
The Texas Ranger's Daughter
Wild West Christmas
A Family for the Rancher
Running Wolf

Harlequin Nocturne

Dream Stalker
Ghost Stalker
Soul Whisperer
Beauty's Beast
The Vampire's Wolf
The Shifter's Choice

Visit the Author Profile page at Harlequin.com.

CAST OF CHARACTERS

Dalton Stevens—NYC undercover detective recovering from a gunshot wound after an attack that killed his partner. His desire to return to active duty has caused his wife to ask for a separation.

Erin Stevens—Outdoor adventure guide and wife of Dalton Stevens, who wants her husband to leave his dangerous job before it kills him. Barring that, she wants a divorce.

Oscar Boyle—Erin's boss at adventure camp.

Henry Larson—A fellow NYC detective and Dalton's trusted friend.

Lawrence Foster—Homeland Security agent.

Rylee Hockings—Homeland Security agent.

Kane Tillerman—CIA operative.

Clint Gabriel—CIA operative.

Vincent Eulich—Member of the terrorist organization Siming's Army, a group of unknown strength embedded in New York State.

Chapter One

On his first day off in three months, Detective Dalton Stevens shouldered his backpack and set out after his wife. He knew she'd be surprised to see him and possibly furious. She'd tell him that trial separations meant the couple separated. Well, the hell with that.

His wife, outdoor adventure specialist Erin Stevens, was up here in the Adirondacks somewhere. He had arrived last night, but as it was dark and he didn't know the location of her guided excursion, he'd had to wait until this morning. That meant she was well ahead of him. It seemed like he'd been chasing after Erin ever since he met her, and the woman knew how to play hard to get. But this time was different. This time he really didn't think she wanted to be caught. She wanted a separation. In his mind, *separation* was just code for *impending divorce*. Well, the hell with that, too.

Dalton adjusted the straps on his shoulders. He couldn't use the padded hip strap because it rubbed against his healing stomach wound.

The group she was leading had already been at it a full day. Normally he could have caught them by now. But nothing was normal since he'd told her he'd been cleared by the department physician to return to active duty.

"Did you hear anything I said?" she'd asked.

"I heard you, Erin," Dalton said to the endless uphill trail. Roots crisscrossed the path, and moss grew on the damp rocks that littered the way. He'd lost his footing twice, and the twisting caused a pain in his middle that made him double over in agony.

Cleared for duty did not mean cleared for hiking with a fifty-pound pack. It would have been lighter if he'd left the tent, but he knew his wife's tent was a single. He'd packed one that suited two. Ever hopeful, he thought. Now if he could just get her in there, he was certain the starlight and the fresh air would clear her mind.

She was always happiest in the outdoors. Erin seemed to glow with health and contentment in this bug-infested, snake-ridden, root-laden wilderness. Meanwhile, he couldn't tell poison ivy from fern, and the last time he'd carried a pack was in Afghanistan.

He stopped again to catch his breath, drawing out his mobile phone and finding he still had no service.

"Nature," he scoffed. He'd take a neighborhood with a quality pizza joint any day.

Erin's boss, and the director of the adult adventure camp, had given him a directions to the trailhead by phone and Dalton had picked up a topographical map. If he was reading this correctly, he should reach their second camping site shortly after they did. Yesterday they had used the kayaks to paddle the Hudson River before stopping for their first camp. This morning they should arrive here to await the scheduled release of water from Lake Abanakee this evening. This area of the Hudson was above the family rafting sites and would be wild running tomorrow, according to the director. The director said he would alert one of the rafting outfits to keep an eye out for him tomorrow, in case he needed a lift downriver.

Meanwhile, this trail from O-K Slip Road was all rocks and roots, and he seemed to catch his feet on each one. Recovery time from abdominal surgery certainly wasn't easy, he thought.

He reached the Hudson Gorge and realized it would be a miracle to find them, even knowing their general stopping point. If they changed the plan and camped on the opposite side, he was out of luck and up the river without a paddle or raft.

Gradually he left the pine forest and moved through birch and maple as he approached the river. He was relieved to finally come upon their camping site knowing she and her group would not be far.

Erin had chosen a rocky outcropping, away from the tall trees and on a covering of moss and grass that spread across the gray rock above the river.

The brightly colored tents were scattered in a rough circle. The trees below the outcropping made it impossible to see them, but he could hear their laughter and raised voices plainly enough.

He didn't see Erin's little single tent because she wouldn't camp very close to her charges. He was certain of that much, because his wife liked her privacy. Perhaps too damn much.

He found her camp in short order and dropped his pack beside her gray-and-white tent.

Erin's pack rested inside the tent, and her food was properly hung in the trees to prevent attracting animals. The peals of laughter and howls of delight guided him to the trail to the river.

A young man and an older woman headed in his direction, winding up the steep path from the water. The route inclined so sharply that the pair clung to saplings as they climbed. The skinny youth wore wet swim trunks and gripped a towel around his neck. His legs were pearly pale, but his face and arms showed a definite sunburn. The woman wore a one-piece bathing suit with jean shorts plastered to her legs and rivulets of water running down her tanned skin.

"Having fun?" Dalton asked.

The youth pointed a toned arm back the way they had come. "There's a rock like a diving board down there. Water's deep and still. It's awesome!"

The woman held her smile as her brows lifted in surprise. "Well, hey there. Didn't see another paddler."

He thumbed over his shoulder. "Came overland. The trail from O-K Slip Road."

She passed him going in the opposite direction. "Well, that's no fun."

He stepped off the trail to let them pass and continued, landing on his backside with a jolt of pain more than once.

"No fun is right," he muttered.

At the bank of the river, he saw the three remaining adult campers and their leader. He'd recognize those legs anywhere. Firm tanned legs pushing off the gray rock as she climbed, leaving wet footprints from her water shoes as she easily scaled the boulder that was shaped like the fin of a shark, using a climbing rope. It was his wife.

On the pinnacle of the sloping boulder she waited for a young woman in a pink bathing suit, which was an unfortunate match to her ruddy skin tone, to jump off and then followed behind, giving a howl of delight that made Dalton frown. He'd never heard her make such a sound of pure exhilaration.

The single male waded out of the water and came up short at the sight of him. Dalton judged the man to be early twenties and carrying extra pounds around his middle.

"Hiya," he said.

Dalton nodded and the young man crept past him on the uneven bank. The woman in pink swam and then waded after the man, followed by a lanky female with wet hair so short it stood up like a hedgehog's spines. Erin emerged from her underwater swim at the base of the rock, scaling the slope to retrieve her climbing rope before making a final leap with the coiled rope over one shoulder.

Dalton smiled as the pinkish woman, her face red from exertion, reached the muddy shore, her cheeks puffing out with each breath.

"Where'd you...come...from?" she wheezed.

"Your camp."

She gave him a skeptical look and paused, one hand on her knee.

"You don't look like an adventure camper."

"No?" He grinned. "What do I look like?"

She cocked her head and her eyes narrowed. "A soldier."

That surprised him as he had once been just that. But he'd left Special Forces at Erin's request.

"Why's that?"

She pointed at the hunting knife that he'd strapped to his belt and then to his boots, military issue and which still fit. Finally, she lifted her finger to the tattoos staining his left forearm from wrist to elbow. The overall pattern spoke of lost comrades, blood, war dead and the corps.

"You sure you're with us?"

"Erin's my wife."

Her entire demeanor changed. Her face brightened and the look of suspicion vanished.

"Oh, hi! I'm Alice. Your wife, she's wonderful. So encouraging and warm." Her smile faltered. "You're her husband?"

He didn't like the incredulity in her voice.

"Yeah." For now. His stomach gave a twist that had nothing to do with healing tissue.

"Hmm. Can't see it."

"Why?"

"She's fun and you're, well, you seem kinda… serious, you know?"

His brows sank deeper over his eyes. He was fun.

The woman glanced back down the trail where all but one hiker had vanished. "She didn't mention you."

"Feel free to ask her."

Alice waved. "See you at camp."

She moved past him and continued up the trail with her comrade on her heels. This other woman said nothing, just gave him a sullen look and glanced away the minute they made eye contact.

Erin reached the spot where she changed from swimming in the calm stretch to wading. He waited beside the kayaks.

Her tank top clung to her skin, and he could see the two-piece suit she wore beneath, along with much of her toned, athletic build. Her wet light brown hair, cut bluntly at her jawline, had lost its natural wave in the water. Her whiskey-brown eyes sparkled above her full mouth, now stretched wide in a playful grin. He took a moment to admire the view of his wife, wet and smiling.

He had the sudden impulse to hide before she spotted him.

Dalton didn't know how Erin knew he was there,

but she straightened, giving him a moment to study her standing alert and relaxed as if listening to the birds that flitted across the water. Then she turned and her eyes shifted to her husband. The set of her jaw told him that she was not pleased.

Dalton was six-three and weighed 245 pounds, but Erin's scowl made him feel about two feet tall.

"Surprise?" he said, stretching his arms out from his sides in a ta-da posture.

Her gaze flicked to his middle, where she knew he still wore a bandage though the stitches were out now. She didn't manage to keep from uttering a profanity. He knew this because he read it on her lips. The Lord's name...in vain. Definitely. Then she tucked in her chin and started marching toward him in a way that would have made a lesser man run. Instead, he slid his hands into the rear pockets of his cargo pants and forced a smile that felt as awkward as a middle school slow dance.

"Dalton, if that's you, you had better run."

He did, running toward her, meeting her as she reached the bank.

He stopped before her, then reached, preparing to swing her in a circle, as he did after separations of more than a day.

She pressed her palm against the center of his chest and extended her arm, blocking him. "Don't you dare lift me. You shouldn't be lifting anything."

He was suddenly glad he'd dumped his pack.

She hoisted the coiled rope farther up on her

shoulder and aimed her extended finger at him. Her scowl deepened and her gaze shot back to him. "How long have you been tracking me?"

"Just today. I signed up for your group."

Her fists went to her hips. "So I couldn't send you home, right?"

Her two female adults had not climbed up to camp, opting to linger and watch the awkward reunion. Dalton glared, but they held their position, their heads swiveling from her to him as they awaited his reply, reminding him of spectators at a tennis match. Dalton pinned his eyes on his wife, an opponent, wishing they were alone but knowing that the women bearing witness might just play in his favor. Erin's tone was icy, but she had not raised it...yet.

He grinned, leaned in for a kiss and caught only her cheek as she stepped back, scowling.

"I can't believe this," she muttered, pushing past him and heading up the trail. Her campers scuttled ahead of them and out of sight.

He trotted after her, ignoring the tug of pain that accompanied each stride.

"Did you bring a kayak?" she asked.

"No."

"You planning on swimming the rapids tomorrow?"

"I thought you'd be happy."

She kept walking, leaning against the slope. Her calf muscles were tight, and he pictured those ankles locked about his lower back. It had been too long.

"I'm taking a vacation. Just like you wanted," he added.

She spun and stormed a few steps away, and then she rounded on him.

"You didn't hear a word I said back there." She pointed toward a tree that he assumed was in the direction of Yonkers, New York, and their pretty little split ranch house with the yard facing woods owned by the power company and a grill on the patio that he had planned to use over the July Fourth weekend. Instead, he was adventure camping without a kayak.

She continued, voice raised. "A vacation? Is that what you got from our last conversation?"

"I missed you." He held his grin, but felt it dying at the edges. Drying up like a dead lizard in the sun. She didn't look back.

"You told me you understood. That you'd take this time to think..." She turned and tapped a finger on his forehead as if to check that there was anyone home. "Really think, about my concerns."

"You said a break."

"You knew exactly what kind of a break I wanted. But, instead, you went for the grand gesture. Like always."

He reached to cup her cheek, but she dodged and his arm dropped to his side. "Honey, listen..."

She looked up at him with disappointment, the hill not quite evening their heights. Then she placed a hand over his, and for a minute he thought it would be all right. Her eyes squeezed shut and a tear dribbled down her cheek.

Dalton gasped. He was making her cry. Erin didn't cry unless she was furious.

The pinkish woman appeared at the edge of the meadow, stepping beside them as her eyes shifted back and forth between them. She tugged on her thick rope of a braid as if trying to decide whether she should proceed or speak.

Dalton looked at his wife. She hadn't kissed him. When was the last time that she had greeted him without a kiss?

When she'd left for adventure camp yesterday, he recalled.

An icy dread crystallized around his heart. He would not lose her. Everything was changing. He had to figure out how to change it back. Change her back.

"Erin, come on," he coaxed.

She was listening, and so was the interloper. He turned to the camper.

"Seriously?" he said, and she scuttled away toward the others, who all stood together facing him and their camp leader, his wife.

Erin faced her group. "This man is my husband, Dalton," she said. "I wasn't expecting him."

The assemble stood motionless, only their eyes flicking from him to her.

Erin growled and strode away. She reached her tent, paused at the sight of his pack and dropped the rope. Her hands went to her hips. She turned to glare at him. He swallowed.

When he gave her his best smile, she closed her eyes and turned away. Then she stripped out of her tank top and into a dry sweatshirt, leaving her wet suit on underneath. He tried to hide his disappointment as she dragged on dry shorts. She spoke, it seemed, to her pack.

"If you were listening, you would have respected my wishes."

"I heard everything you said. I did. I just..." *Ignored you*, he thought, but wisely stopped speaking.

"I don't think listening is enough."

"What does that even mean?"

"You always listen to me, Dalton. And then you do as you darn well please. My feelings don't change your decisions. They don't even seem to weigh into your thought process anymore. You want to go on living like you always have, and that's your right. And it's my right to step off the roller coaster."

"Is *stepping off the roller coaster* punishment, Erin? Is that what you're trying to do? Is that why you left?"

"I can't talk to you here. I'm working."

"I'll wait."

"It won't matter how long you wait, Dalton. You don't want to change."

"Because everything is fine just the way it is."

"No, Dalton. It isn't."

The way she said "it isn't" froze his blood. The

flat, defeated tone left no doubt that she was ready to cut him loose.

Erin opened her mouth to speak, but instead cocked her head. A moment later she had her hand shielding her eyes as she glanced up toward the sky. Her hearing was better than his.

He'd fired too many shots with his M4 rifle without ear protection over in Afghanistan. So he followed the direction of Erin's attention and, a moment later, made out the familiar thumping drone of the blades of a helicopter.

"That's funny," Erin said.

The chopper broke the ridgeline across the river, wobbling dangerously and issuing black smoke from the tail section.

Dalton judged the angle of descent and the length of the meadow. The pilot was aiming for this flat stretch of ground beyond the tents that ringed the clearing. Dalton knew it would be a hard landing.

He grabbed Erin, capturing her hand, and yanked her toward the trees. In the meadow, standing like startled deer amid their colorful tents, her charges watched the approaching disaster in petrified stillness.

"Take cover!" he shouted, still running with his wife. "Get down!"

Chapter Two

Erin cried out in horror as the rails below the chopper snapped the treetops above them. Branches rained down from the sky, and Dalton dragged her against him as the roar of the engine seemed to pass directly over her head. She squeezed her eyes shut as her rib cage shuddered with the terrible vibrations of the whirling blades.

She opened her eyes as the chopper tipped in the air, the blades now on their side rotating toward her and churning upright like a window fan gone mad. It was going to hit the ground, blades first, right there before her.

In the meadow, Brian Peters, the skinny seventeen-year-old who was here because his father wanted him away from his computers for a week, was now running for his life. She judged he'd clear the descending blade but feared the fuselage would crush him. Brian's acne-scarred cheeks puffed as he bolted, lanky and loose limbed. Behind him Merle Levine, the oldest of her group, a square and solidly built woman in her late fifties, lay prone beside her cheery red tent with her arms folded over her head. Merle was a single biology teacher on summer vacation and directly in the path Erin feared the chopper would take as it hit the ground.

Erin squeezed her face between open palms as the propeller caught. Instead of plowing into the earth, the helicopter cartwheeled as the blades sheered and folded under the momentum of the crash.

Erin saw Carol Walton lift her arms and then fall as debris swept her off her feet. The timid woman had reminded Erin of a porcupine, with small close-set eyes and spiky bleached hair tufted with black. Erin's scream mingled with Carol's as the woman vanished from sight.

The chopper careened toward the escarpment, some twenty feet above the river just beyond the meadow. The entire craft slowed and then tipped before scraping across the rock with exquisite slowness.

Richard Franklin, a twentysomething craft beer brewer from Oklahoma, was already close to the edge and he stood, watching the chopper as it teetered. He reached out toward the ruined aircraft and Erin realized he could see whoever was aboard. Then he ran as if to catch the two-ton machine in his pale outstretched arms. The chopper fell over the cliff and Richard dropped to his posterior.

Erin scanned the ground for the flash of a pink bathing suit. "Where's Alice?"

Not a bird chirped or squirrel scuttled. The wind

had ceased and all insects stilled. The group rose, as one, staring and bug-eyed. The sudden quiet was deafening. They began to walk in slow zombie-like synchronicity toward the spot where the helicopter had vanished. All except for Dalton.

Dalton released Erin and charged toward the spot where Carol Walton knelt, folded in the middle and clutching her belly like an opera soprano in the final act. Only Erin knew the blood was real.

Alice Afton appeared beside her, having obviously been hiding in the woods.

"Alice, get my pack. There's a med kit in there," Erin said.

Alice trotted off and Erin moved on wooden legs toward Carol Walton, knowing from the amount of blood spilling from her wounds that she could not survive.

Dalton cradled Carol in his lap, and her head lay in the crook of his elbow. In different circumstances the hold would seem that of a lover. His short, dark brown hair, longer on top, fell forward over his broad forehead, covering his heavy brows and shielding the green eyes that she knew turned amber near the iris. She could see the nostrils of his broad nose flare as he spoke.

"I got you," said Dalton. "Don't you worry."

"Tell my mom, I love her," said Carol.

Erin realized then that Carol knew she was dying. But there was none of the wild panic she had expected. Carol stared up at Dalton as if knowing he would guide her to where she needed to go. The confidence he projected, the experience. How many of his fellow marines had he held just like this?

Army never leaves their wounded. Marines never leave their dead.

"Can I do anything?" asked Erin. She couldn't. Nothing that would keep Carol with them.

"Take her hand," he said in a voice that was part exasperation, part anguish. She knew he'd lost comrades in war and it bothered him deeply.

Erin did, and warm blood coated her palm.

Alice arrived, panting, and extended the pack.

"Just put it down for now," said Dalton, his voice calm.

"Why doesn't it hurt?" asked Carol, lowering her chin as if to look at the slicing belly wound. Something had torn her from one side to the other and the smell of her compromised bowels made Erin gag.

But not Dalton. He lifted Carol's chin with two fingers and said. "Hey, look at me. Okay?"

Carol blinked up at him. "She's a lucky woman, your wife. Does she know that?"

Dalton smiled, stroking her head. "Sometimes."

Carol's color changed from ashen to blue. She shivered and her eyes went out of focus. Then her breathing changed. She gasped and her body went slack.

Dalton checked the pulse at her throat as Erin's vision blurred. He shook his head and whispered, "Gone."

From the lip of the cliff, Brian Peters called. "I can see someone moving down there."

Dalton slipped out from under Carol's slack body and rose. He glanced down at Erin, and she pressed her lips together to keep from crying.

"Come on," he said, and headed toward the rocky outcropping.

He tugged her to her feet and she hesitated, eyes still pinned on the savaged corpse that was Carol Walton just a few minutes ago.

"Erin. We have to see about the crew." His voice held authority.

How was he so calm? she wondered, but merely nodded her head and allowed him to hurry her along, like an unwilling dog on a leash.

And then, there they were on the lip of rock that jutted out over the Hudson. Twenty feet below them the ruined helicopter lay, minus its blades. One of the runners was snagged over a logjam that held the ruined chopper as the bubble of clear plastic slowly filled with river water. Inside the pilot slumped in his seat, tethered in place by the shoulder restraints.

"Is he alone?" asked Merle, coming to stand beside Dalton, asking him the questions as he emerged as the clear leader of their party.

"Seems so," said Dalton as he released Erin's hand.

"He's moving!" said Richard, pointing a finger at the river.

Erin craned her neck and saw the pilot's head turn to one side. Alive, she realized.

"He's sinking," said Brian. "It's at his feet now."

"We have to get him out of there," said Alice.

"He'll drown," added Richard.

"You have rope?" asked Dalton.

Erin roused from her waking nightmare, knowing exactly what her husband planned. He'd string some rope up and swing down there like Tarzan in a daring rescue attempt.

Except she was the better swimmer. Dalton was only an average swimmer at best and today he was four weeks post-surgery. His abdominal muscles could not handle this. He'd tear something loose, probably the artery that the surgeon had somehow managed to close. She squared her shoulders and faced him.

Erin regained control of her party.

"You are not going down there!" she said.

He ignored her and lifted a hand to snap his fingers before Richard's face. "Rope?"

Richard startled, tore his gaze from the drama unfolding in the river and then hurried off.

"Dalton, I'm the party leader. I'm going," she said.

He smiled at her. "Honey…"

Her eyes narrowed at the placating tone as she interrupted. "You might get down there, but you can't climb back up. Who's going to haul you back?"

He glanced at the drop and the chopper. The water now reached the pilot's knees.

When Richard returned with the gear bag, Erin dropped to the ground and unzipped the duffel. As she removed the throw line and sash cord, she kept talking.

"I'm a better climber. More experienced." She reached in the bag, removed a rope and dropped it at his feet. "Tie a bowline," she said, requesting a simple beginner knot.

His eyes narrowed.

She held up an ascender used to make climbing up a single belay rope as easy as using a StairMaster. "What's this for?" she asked, testing his knowledge of climbing.

His jaw tightened.

"Exactly. I'm going. That's all."

Erin showed Dalton the throw ball, a sand-filled pouch that looked like a cross between a hacky sack and a leather beanbag filled with lead shot. Its purpose was to carry the lighter sash cord up and over tree branches, or in this case, down and around the top of the chopper's damaged rotor. Finished, she rose and offered the throw ball and towline to Dalton because he was better at throwing and because she needed him to leave her alone so she could work.

"Knock yourself out," she said, leaving him to try to snag the helicopter as she slipped into her climbing harness and fastened the chin strap on her helmet.

"How deep is the river here?" asked Dalton.

"Twenty feet, maybe. The river is deeper and wider here, which is why there's no white water. The gorges close back in farther down and the water gets interesting again."

Twenty feet was deep enough to sink that fuselage, she thought.

Erin selected a gap in the top of the rocky outcropping for her chock. This was an aluminum wedge that would hold her climbing rope. The climbing rope, on which she would belay, or use to descend and then return, was strong and much thicker than the towrope, which was no wider than a clothesline. Belaying to the pilot meant using this stronger rope and the cliff wall to drop to his position and then return using two ascenders. The ascenders fixed to the rope and would move only in one direction—up. The ascenders included feet loops, so she could rest on one as she moved the other upward.

She set the wedge in place and then set up her belay system. Finally, she attached her harness to the rope with a carabiner and figure eight belay device. She liked old-school equipment. Simple was best.

By the time she finished collecting all her gear, a second harness and the pack with the first aid kit, Dalton had succeeded in snagging the chopper with the throw ball and pulled the cord tight.

"Got it." He turned to her and grinned, showing her the tight towline.

"Fantastic," she said, squatting at the lip of the cliff. Then she fell backward. She had the satisfaction of seeing the shock on Dalton's face before he disappeared from her sight. Only momentarily, unfortunately. When she glanced up he was scowling down at her. Holding the towrope aloft.

"What's this even for?" he shouted.

"It's like those spinner things, only for grown men."

She continued her descent, smoothly releasing the rope and slowing as she reached the river's uneasy surface. As she approached the chopper, she realized the wreckage was moving, inching back as the rotor dragged along the branch anchoring it in place.

The pressure of the water splashed over the dome in front of the pilot, who turned his head to look up at her. She could see little of the man except that his headphones had fallen over his nose and there was blood, obscured from above by his dark clothing.

Her feet bumped the Plexiglas dome and she held herself in place, dancing sideways on her line to reach the door on the downriver side. It was partially submerged, but the other one took the full force of the current. She'd never be able to open it.

The pilot clutched his middle and turned to the empty seat beside him. He grabbed a red nylon cooler and laboriously moved it to his lap.

"I'm going to get you out," said Erin, doubting that she really could.

Chapter Three

Dalton watched in horror as his wife opened the side compartment door and gave herself enough slack to enter the ruptured compartment of the wrecked chopper.

The pilot lifted his head toward her as she perched on the passenger's seat, now pitched at an odd angle. Her added weight had caused the chopper's runner to farther slip along the anchoring branch. When the chopper tore loose, it would sink and she might be snagged. Cold dread constricted Dalton's chest as he watched helplessly from above.

If he had been the one down there, he was certain the chopper would already have broken loose. She'd been right to go, though he'd still rather switch places with her. She'd been so darn quick with those ropes. Erin knew he was capable of belaying down a rope. And he could climb back up on a good day, but he didn't know how to use the gizmos she had in that pack on her back and jangling from her harness. And today was not a good day.

Beside him, the four surviving campers lay on their bellies and knelt on the rock, all eyes fixed on the drama unfolding below.

The pilot was pushing something toward Erin; it looked like a small red bag. Erin was unbuckling his restraints and shoving the harness behind his back.

The water foaming around the wreckage drowned out their words.

Erin succeeded in getting the waist buckle of the climbing harness clipped about him and was working on tugging the nylon straps of his harness under his legs as the pilot's head lolled back. Erin glanced up at Dalton, a frown on her lips as she exited the compartment and retrieved the towline he had thrown. She was signaling to him with the rope. Pantomiming a knot.

"She wants you to tie a climbing rope to the line," said the older woman "I'm Merle, by the way. I used to do a lot of rock climbing before I got pins in my ankle."

She lifted the coiled climbing rope, expertly connected it through an anchored pulley that she tied to a tree some five feet from the edge, and then tied the larger belay line to the towline. Finally, she signaled to Erin. A moment later Erin was hauling the towline back down, dragging the connected larger rope through the pulley. She continued this until she grasped the belay rope, at which point she quickly tied a loop through which she connected the belay rope to the pilot's harness with a carabiner. Erin removed the pilot's headphones and fitted her own helmet to his head.

Merle lifted the other end of the line, which ran through the pulley secured to the tree trunk, and returned to the rock ledge.

"Take this a minute." Merle offered Dalton the rope. "I know I can't haul that guy up." She then motioned to the others. "Brian, Alice, Richard, come take hold. We'll act like a mule team. Walk that way when I tell you. Slowly." She folded the rope back on itself and tied a series of loops every few feet. Then the others took hold.

Dalton dragged his hand across his throat while simultaneously shaking his head. This, of course, had no effect on his wife who offered a thumbs-up and then used her strong legs to haul the pilot toward the open side door. For a moment the pilot tried again to get Erin to take the red squarish nylon bag. When Erin rejected his attempts to make her take it from him, he gripped the seat, foiling her attempts to remove him from the compartment. Finally, Erin looped the small container over her arm using the black nylon strap. Only then did the pilot assist in his extraction.

Merle extended an arm and pointed at the struggling pair.

"It's moving!"

Dalton shifted his attention from his wife to the helicopter runner. He watched in horror as the twisted remains of one blade slipped free from the branch. In a single heartbeat, the compartment vanished beneath the surface, leaving the pilot, in Erin's helmet, dangling from the rope, half in and half out of the water. With his legs submerged, the pilot was dragged downriver.

Erin's rope went taut. Dalton's breathing stopped as he gripped his wife's rope from the surface of the rock before him and wrapped it behind his legs. He hadn't done this since he was in active duty. He remembered how to anchor a climber, but he had never had to anchor a climber who was below him. Dalton sat into the rope and pulled.

Merle shouted from behind him. "Pull!"

The pilot began to rise, his legs clearing the churning torrent.

Dalton ignored the pain of his healing abdominal muscles as he succeeded in inching back from the edge. How long could Erin hold her breath? What if she was snagged on something in that compartment? The rope stretched tight as if tied down at the other end. He scanned the water for some sight of her, fearing the chopper had rolled onto her line or, worse, onto Erin.

The rope vibrated. Was the fuselage settling or was that his wife moving? Dalton smelled the fear on his perspiration. If the compartment tipped to that side, she would have no escape. She'd be pinned between the compartment and the bottom. Dalton considered his chances of moving upriver and jumping into the water. He made the calculation and came back with the answer. He had zero chance of succeeding. The river would whisk him past the wreck before he could reach her.

Just then he saw movement on the line. He stepped closer to the edge and a hand submerged again as the pilot rose closer to the lip of rock where he stood.

Dalton tugged and Erin's hand appeared again. She clutched something; it looked like a metallic gold coffee mug handle. She slid the handle up the rope and her head emerged.

"She's using an ascender," called Merle. "Two! Holy cow, she set that up underwater? Your wife is magnificent. If I was ten years younger I'd steal that woman."

He saw her then, first her arms, sliding the ascenders along the taut rope. One ascender slid upward and her head cleared the water. Wet hair clung to her red face as she gasped. Her opposite hand appeared, moving upward while gripping the second ascender. The device fixed to a carabiner and then to a sling that she had somehow clipped to her harness. In other words, Erin had released her original attachment to the line and then succeeded in attaching two ascenders and slings to the free portion of the rope all while underwater.

Magnificent was an understatement.

Her torso cleared the water and he saw that the red nylon bag still hung from her shoulder, clamped between her upper arm and side.

"Keep going," called Merle to the pull team as the

pilot appeared beside her and was dragged up onto the flat expanse of rock.

Fifteen feet below him, Erin made progress ascending as he leaned over the edge for a better look at her. This caused the rope to slacken and for Erin to drop several inches. Dalton straightened and sat into the rope. He lost his view of his wife, but Merle called the remaining distance to the top as the pilot's pull team, having finished their job, abandoned their posts to run to the pilot who was struggling to move.

"Five feet," called Merle, motioning him to hold position. Merle extended her hand and Erin gripped it, sliding the opposite ascender into Dalton's line of sight. Then she scrambled up onto the rock, rising to stand before them.

She didn't even look out of breath. He, on the other hand, had lost his wind. Seeing her disappear had broken something loose inside him, and his legs gave way. He collapsed onto the moss-covered rock as he struggled to keep down the contents of his stomach. The climbing rope fell about Erin's feet, and she released the ascenders that clattered to the stone cliff top.

How had she escaped?

Merle was hugging his wife as Erin laughed. The men patted her on the back, and Alice got a hug as well, weeping loudly so that Erin had to comfort *her*.

"I'm getting you all wet," said Erin, extracting herself from Alice's embrace. She ignored Dalton as she turned to the pilot. "How is he?"

Dalton had a rudimentary field experience with triage and rallied to meet her beside the pilot.

"You okay?" he asked.

She nodded, still not looking at him. "Thanks for your help."

But she hadn't needed it or him. All he had done was dunk her as she emerged and possibly speed her arrival slightly by keeping the rope tight.

"Did you get pinned?" he asked.

"Just the rope."

"How did you get out?" he asked.

"Later," she said, and set aside the bag that he now saw was a red nylon lunch cooler. Why had the pilot been so insistent that she retrieve it?

Illegal possibilities rose in his law-enforcement mind, but he turned his attention to the injured man, checking his pupils and pulse.

"Where's your pack?" he asked her.

"Dumped it. Couldn't fit out the side window."

Erin dropped to her knees beside the pilot.

"Shock," he said. At the very least. If he had to guess, and he did have to, because there was no medical help for miles, he'd say the man was bleeding internally. He took a knee beside her and pressed on the pilot's stomach with his fingertips and found the man's skin over the abdominal cavity was tight and the cavity rigid.

"His leg is broken," said Merle, pointing at the

pilot's foot, which was facing in the wrong direction for a man lying on his back.

So is his spleen, thought Dalton.

Chapter Four

"I don't like the sound of his breathing," said Erin, her brow as wrinkled as her wet tank top.

The pilot wheezed now, struggling for breath. His eyes fluttered open.

"Captain Lewis, this is my husband. He's a New York City detective. You wanted to speak to him?" The pilot had given them his name but little else.

The captain nodded. "Just you two," he said, lifting his chin toward the curious faces surrounding him.

Erin pointed at Merle. "Please go find my pack and get my phone. Then call for help. Brian, go find something to cover Carol up with and, Alice and Richard, can you gather my climbing gear?"

The campers scurried away.

"Now, Captain Lewis," said Erin. "What in this cooler is so important that you were willing to kill us both?"

Lewis turned to Dalton and spoke in a guttural whisper. "I work for the Department of Homeland

Security. Orders to collect this and transfer same to a plane bound for the CDC in Virginia."

Dalton felt the hairs on his neck lifting, as if his skin were electrified. The mention of the CDC or Centers for Disease Control indicated to him that whatever was inside was related to infection or disease.

"What's in there?" he asked, aiming an index finger at the bag.

"Flash drive with intel on terrorist cells within the state. Siming's Army, and those vials hold one of the three Deathbringers."

"The what?" asked Dalton.

"I don't know, exactly. Mission objective was to pick up a package, which contains an active virus—a deadly one—and the vaccine."

Erin moved farther from the cooler that had been dangling recently from her arm.

"So it's dangerous?" she asked.

"Yes, ma'am. Deadly. You have to get it to DHS or the FBI. Don't trust anyone else."

"Who shot you down?" Dalton had seen the bullet holes in the fuselage.

"Foreign agents. Mercenaries. Don't know. Whoever they are, they work for Siming's Army. And more will be coming to recover that." He pointed at the cooler.

"Where'd you get it?" asked Dalton.

"An operative. Agent Ryan Carr. Use his name. Get as far from here as possible."

"But you're injured," said Erin.

"No, ma'am. I'm dying." He glanced to Dalton, who nodded his agreement.

"Internal injuries," said Dalton through gritted teeth. Two deaths, and he'd been unable to do a damned thing to save them.

"I thank you for pulling me out. You two have to complete my mission."

"No," said Erin at the same time Dalton said, "Yes."

She stared at him. "I can't leave these people out here and I'm not taking charge of a deadly anything."

The captain spoke to her, slipping his hand into hers.

"It's a dying man's last request."

She tried to pull back. "That's not fair."

He grinned and then wheezed. His breath smelled of blood. "All's fair in love and war."

He used the other hand to push the cooler toward Dalton, who accepted the package.

She pointed at the red nylon travel cooler. "Dalton, do not take that."

But he already had.

"Get him a blanket, Erin. He's shivering."

She stood and glared at him, then hurried off.

Dalton stayed with the captain as he grew paler and his eyes went out of focus. He'd seen this before. Too many times, but this time the blood stayed politely inside his dying body. The pilot's belly swelled with it and so did his thigh. The broken femur had cut some blood supply, Dalton was certain, from the lack of pulse at the pilot's ankle and the way his left pant leg was now so tight.

"Tell my girlfriend, Sally, that I was fixing to ask for her hand. Tell her I love her and I'm sorry."

"I'll tell her." If he lived to see this through. Judging from the number of bullet holes in that chopper and the size of the caliber, staying alive was going to be a challenge.

Erin returned with her down sleeping bag and draped it over the shivering captain. Before the sun reached the treetops as it dipped into the west, the captain joined Carol Walton in death.

Dalton stood. "We have to go."

"Go? Go where? I've got two dead bodies and responsibility for the welfare of my group. I can't just leave them."

No, they couldn't just leave them. But there were few safe choices. Traveling as a group would be slow. "Get the kayaks ready. We're going."

"I am not taking this group into river rapids ninety minutes before sunset. Are you crazy?"

"Not as crazy as meeting them here." He motioned to the open field.

"Meeting who?" she asked.

"Siming's Army."

Twenty minutes later Erin, now in dry clothing, gathered the surviving campers and explained that the captain's helicopter was shot down, he claimed, by terrorists who would be coming for whatever was in that bag. She explained that leaving this evening was hazardous because of the volume of water at the forefront of the scheduled release from Lake Abanakee. Finally, she relayed that it was her husband's belief that they needed to leave this site immediately.

"I'm for that. Staying the night with two dead bodies gives me the creeps," said Brian.

"You can't just leave them out here for the predators," said Richard.

"You rather be here when the predators show up?" asked Merle.

"We called for help. They are sending an air rescue team for them," Brian said. "We should at least wait until they pick up the dead."

"We wait, there will be more dead," said Dalton.

"What do you think, Erin?" asked Brian.

"I would prefer to stay put and wait for help."

"What's coming isn't help," said Dalton.

ON EMPTY STOMACHS, the campers packed up their tents and gear, while Erin and Dalton headed down the rocky outcropping to ready the kayaks that had been stowed for their excursion the following morning. Dalton took Carol's gear and kayak.

"You really sure about this?" asked Erin, her gaze flicking from Dalton, who carried one end of Carol's kayak, and then to the frothing river behind him.

"Sure about our responsibility to deliver this? Yes."

"Sure about taking inexperienced kayakers into

the roughest stretch of white water one hour before sunset. What if someone upends?"

He lowered the kayak onto the grassy bank. "What would you normally do?"

"Pick them up from the river and guide them to shore."

"We'll do that."

"In the dark?"

"You're right. We can't do that."

"So your plan is to leave anyone who gets into trouble. And here I thought you were the hero type."

That stung. He wouldn't leave anyone behind. She had to know that. "Erin, he said they're coming. Mercenaries. You understand? That means hired killers, and I know they are using high-caliber rounds from the size of the holes in the tail section of the chopper. We can argue later about specific logistics. Right now we need to…"

She was cocking her head again. Looking toward the sky. He didn't hear it yet, not over the roar of the river. But he knew what was coming.

Dalton looked at the three kayaks they had retrieved from cover. Her gear lay beside her craft, neatly stowed in her pack. Dalton slipped her gear into the hollow forward compartment of her craft and added her paddle so that it rested half in and half out of the opening.

Erin arched backward, staring up at the pink sky with her hand acting as visor. Dalton packed his gear into the bow of Carol Walton's craft and added the red nylon cooler, which now contained nothing but a river rock. The black case, recently within, held two small vials in a padded black compartment with a thumb drive. This precious parcel now rested safely in the side pocket of his cargo pants.

"They're here," she said, pointing at the red-and-white helicopter with Rescue emblazoned on the side.

The chopper hovered over the meadow, then began a measured descent. Erin stepped back toward the tree-lined trail that led to the meadow. Dalton glanced at the kayaks, packed and ready, and just knew he'd never get her to go without her group.

So he abandoned their escape plan and followed her. He could at least see that she wasn't one of the welcome party.

Dalton made sure he was beside her when they reached the sharply ascending trailhead at the edge of the open field. Before them, the chopper had landed. The pilot cut the engine and the copilot stepped down. Dalton studied the man. He wore aviator glasses, slacks and a button-up shirt. Nothing identified him as mountain rescue and his smile seemed out of place. As he crouched and trotted beneath the slowing blades that whirled above him, Dalton spotted the grip of a pistol tucked in the back of his slacks.

Erin moved to step from cover and he dragged her back.

"What are you doing?" she said.

He held a finger to his lips. "Wait."

Merle was first to greet the copilot. Their raised voices carried across the meadow.

"How many in your party?" asked the new arrival, straightening now. He was a small man, easy to underestimate, Dalton thought. The relaxed posture seemed crafted, just like his casual attire.

"There are six of us," answered Merle, omitting the two dead.

"Where's the crashed chopper?"

Merle pointed, half-turning to face the river. "Went into the Hudson and sank."

The copilot glanced back to the chopper and the side door slid open. The man within crouched in the opening. There was a familiar metal cylinder over his shoulder and a strap across the checked cotton shirt he wore. Dalton had carried a rifle just like it on many missions while in Special Ops. It was an M4.

"What about the pilot?" asked the newcomer. "He go down with his chopper?"

Brian answered that one, coming to stand beside Merle. "We got him out. But he died."

Dalton groaned.

"Too bad," said the copilot.

Alice smiled brightly, standing in a line beside Brian. The only thing missing was the wall to make this a perfect setup for a firing squad. Dalton had a pistol but it would hardly be a match for three armed mercenaries. They'd kill him and, more importantly, they'd kill Erin. So he waited, backing her up with a firm pull on her arm. They now watched through the cover of pine boughs.

Dalton knew what would happen next. He ran through possibilities of what he could do, if anything, to prevent it.

"Do something," whispered Erin.

"If I do something, they'll know our position."

"They're going to kill them."

"I think so."

"So save them."

"It will endanger you."

"What would you do if I wasn't here?"

He glanced at her. "You *are* here."

Dalton watched from his position. "Get behind that tree." He pointed. "Stay there and when I say run, you run for the kayaks."

"Dalton?"

"Promise me."

She met his gaze and nodded, then stepped behind the thick trunk of the pine tree. He moved beside her.

In the clearing, one of the new arrivals glanced in his direction and then back to Alice.

"You retrieve anything from the craft before it went down?"

"Yeah," said Alice,

Dalton aimed at the one with the rifle.

"What exactly?"

"A red cooler. We have to take it to the FBI," said Brian.

"That so? Where is it now, exactly?"

Brian seemed to have realized that he faced a wolf in sheep's clothing because he rested a hand on his neck and rubbed before speaking.

"Back by our tents," he lied. "I'll get it for you." He turned to go.

The man with the aviator glasses motioned for the pilot to follow. The copilot lifted his hand to signal the shooter. The rifleman raised his weapon and Dalton took his shot, dropping him like a sack of rags.

By the time Dalton swung his pistol away from the dead man, the copilot had Alice in front of him, using her as a human shield.

"Come out or she dies," said their leader.

He didn't, and the man shot Merle and Richard in rapid succession. They fell like wheat before the scythe.

From the brush where Brian had disappeared came the sound of thrashing. Dalton suspected the teen had made a run for it.

The copilot dragged Alice back toward the chopper, using the nose cone as cover, as he shouted to the pilot. Another shot sounded and Alice fell forward to the ground, shot through the head.

"Kill whoever is shooting. Then find the sample," said the copilot.

"The boy?"

"No witnesses."

Dalton leaned toward Erin and whispered, "When they find that cooler, they'll kill us. You understand?"

She nodded.

"Run!"

Erin didn't look back at the carnage. Instead, she fled down the trail toward the river. Dalton had a time trying to keep up.

At the bank of the Hudson, Erin finally came to a halt. She folded at the waist and gripped her knees with both hands, panting.

"They killed them. Just shot them down," she said.

Dalton thought he'd heard his wife express every emotion possible from elation to fury. But this voice, this high reedy thread of a voice, didn't seem to belong to Erin.

"Where's Brian?"

He wouldn't get far with two trained killers on his trail.

Erin, who had just belayed into a river and rescued a wounded man. Who had led this group here to disaster. Who had just watched three more people die. The first deaths she'd ever witnessed.

A sharp threat of worry stitched his insides.

She straightened, and he took in her pale face and bloodless lips. He felt a second jolt of panic. She was going into shock.

"Erin." He took a firm hold of both her elbows and gave a little shake. "We have to go now." Her eyes snapped into focus and she met his gaze. There she was, pale, panting and scared. But she was back.

"Brian," she whispered and then shouted. "Brian!"

He appeared like a lost puppy, crashing through the brush, holding one bleeding arm with his opposite hand.

Behind him came the pilot. Dalton squeezed off two shots, sending his pursuer back into cover.

Erin and Brian crouched on the bank as Erin removed a red bandanna from her pocket and tied it around the bullet wound in the boy's arm.

She closed her mouth and scowled as a familiar fierce expression emerged on her face.

"Those animals are not getting away with this." She glanced toward the trail. His wife was preparing to fight.

"Erin, get into your kayak. Now." He tugged her toward the watercrafts.

She paused and looked at her pack and the paddle already in place for departure. Then she glanced at him.

"You knew?"

"Suspected."

She clutched Brian's good arm. "He can't paddle with one arm." She wiped her hand over her mouth. "And you don't know how to navigate in white water."

True enough.

The kayaks each held only one person. Dalton took another shot to send their attacker back behind the tree.

"He'll have to try," said Dalton.

"Get in, Brian. I'll launch you."

Tears stained the boy's pink, hairless cheeks, and blood stained his forearm, but he climbed into a kayak. Erin handed him a paddle and shoved his craft into the river.

"Now you," she called to him.

He knew what would happen when he stopped shooting. They'd be sitting ducks on the river.

"I'll be right behind you."

"Dalton. No."

"You promised," he said.

Brian was already in the current, struggling to paddle.

"Go," he coaxed, wondering if this was the last time that he'd ever see her.

She went with a backward glance, calling directions as she pushed the kayak into the Hudson.

"Get to the center of the river and avoid the logs. Hug the right shore going into the first turn and the left on the second. How far are we going?"

"Get under cover." They would be sitting ducks on the river once the chopper was airborne. He needed to kill that pilot.

"Got it."

He moved his position as the pilot left cover to fire at what he assumed was three kayakers.

Never assume. Dalton took the shot and the man staggered back to cover.

Body armor, Dalton realized.

He caught a glimpse of the man darting between the trees in retreat. He took another shot, aiming for his head, and missed. Then he climbed into the kayak. Erin's graceful departure had made the launch look easy. His efforts included using the paddle to shove himself forward, nearly upending in the process.

He moved by inches, shocked at how much his abdomen ached as he felt the grass and earth dragging under him. The river snatched him from the shore. He retrieved his double-bladed paddle, glancing forward to catch a glimpse of Erin before she vanished from his view. The pitch and buck of the river seemed a living thing beneath him, and this was the wide, quiet part.

He used his paddle to steer but did not propel himself forward. The river began to churn with the first set of rapids. He rocketed along, propelled by the hydrodynamics of the surging water.

Above him, the sky blazed scarlet, reflecting on the dark water like blood. Erin had never seen a dead body. Today she had seen six.

As if summoned from the twilight by his thoughts, he glimpsed Erin on the far bank, towing Brian's kayak to shore. He tried and failed to redirect her.

Erin reached the rocky shore and leaped out, holding both crafts as Brian struggled from his vessel. He didn't look back as he ran into the woods and vanished.

Dalton shouted as he slipped past her, using his paddle in an ineffective effort to reverse against the current.

He still splashed and shouted when Erin appeared again, towing an empty kayak. She darted past him, her paddle flashing silver in the fading light. She took point and he fell in behind her, mirroring her strokes and ignoring the painful tug in his middle that accompanied each pull of the blade through the surging water. She hugged the first turn just as she'd instructed him and he tried to follow, but swept wider and nearly hit the boulder cutting the water like the fin of a tiger shark.

She glanced back and shouted something inaudible, and they sped through a churning descent that made his stomach pitch as river water splashed into his vessel's compartment. He could hear nothing past the roar of the white water, and neither could Erin. He knew this because he spotted the second turn in the river at the same moment he caught the flash of the red underbelly of the helicopter.

Erin's head lifted as the chopper swept over them and took a position downriver, hovering low and then dropping out of sight. It would be waiting, he knew, low over the water to pick them off when they made the next turn.

Hug the right shore on the first turn and the left on the second. That was what she had told him, but his wife was very clearly making a path to the right on this second turn.

Dalton struggled to follow against the pull of the river that tried to drag him left. On the turn he saw the reason for her warning. There before him loomed the largest logjam of downed trees he'd ever seen, and it rushed right at them. Waves hit the barrier and soared ten feet in the air, soaking the logs that choked the right bank of the turn. The pile of debris seemed injected with towering pillars of rock.

It occurred to him then why most groups did not run this section of the river and never after a release from the dam.

Erin performed a neat half turn, riding a wave partially up the natural dam as the second kayak flipped. The river dropped her back and she pulled until she grasped a branch near the shore. She held on as the river tore the empty craft from hers. The empty vessel bobbed up beyond the logs and sped downriver as Erin struggled to keep hers from being dragged under the web of branches.

He tried to mimic her maneuver but instead rammed bow-first into the nest of branches. The water lifted the back of his kayak while forcing the bow down and under the debris.

"Grab hold," Erin yelled.

He did, managing to grip the slimy, lichen-covered limb as the kayak continued its path downward and into the debris. He used both feet to snag the shoulder straps of his pack as his watercraft vanished beneath him. His stomach burned and he knew he could hold his pack or the limb, but not both. His current physical weakness infuriated him, but he dropped his pack. It fell to his seat in front of the red cooler decoy. Both his gear and the kayak were pulled under.

He hauled himself farther up on the debris as his kayak resurfaced beyond the fallen tree limb where he clung and his craft was whisked away.

He sighed at the loss, but with his feet free he could now climb to a spot above where Erin was snagged. He help move the nose of her craft back and clear of a branch. Then she dragged and pulled herself toward the shore. Just a little farther and the current calmed. Erin shoved with her paddle and reached the shallows as he scrambled beside the log dam.

How many seconds until the chopper realized they were no longer on the river?

Chapter Five

Erin clambered onto shore, pausing only to tug her backpack from the inner compartment. Dalton dropped from the brush pile to land in the shallows beside her and dragged her kayak off the shore and well into the cover of the pines before halting to look back at the river.

No one ran that portion of the river on the day of a planned release. The water was too deep and too fast. She was shocked she hadn't rolled under the mass of twisted branches. Even experienced paddlers could be pinned by rolling water or submerged obstacles.

She looked back at the river now thirty feet behind them. The sound of rushing water abated. The roar lessened to a churning tumble, like a waterfall.

By slow degrees, the sound changed to something mechanical. The whirling of the chopper blades, she realized.

The killers had waited long enough. They were coming upriver.

Erin shouldered the second strap of her pack and

crouched down as the helicopter swept low over the water, heading upriver. Dalton paused for its passing, then grabbed the towrope and hauled the kayak farther back into the woods until he and her vessel disappeared.

The helicopter raced past again and then hovered over the brush pile. Could they see Dalton's pack or his kayak? They definitely saw something.

How was this even happening?

Was Brian all right? He couldn't paddle with his wounded arm and she knew she'd never navigate the rapids towing him. The choice was hard, but leaving him gave him his best chance. They wouldn't know where or on which side of the river to find him. His wound was serious but he could walk, run actually.

Run and hide. When they're gone, when you're certain, you can find the river trail. The blue trail. Follow it upriver to the road.

He'd understood, she was sure, but with his pale cheeks and the shock, she didn't know if he could make it to safety.

"Please let him be all right," she whispered.

If her muscles didn't ache and her teeth weren't chattering, she'd try to chalk this up as some bad dream. Instead, it was a full-fledged nightmare. A waking one.

Her mind flashed on an image of Carol Walton, her stomach torn open by a soulless piece of debris that could have struck any one of them. Erin covered her eyes, but the image remained, emblazoned in her mind. That flying metal could have killed Dalton just as easily as Carol. And then she'd be dead in that meadow with her entire outdoor adventure group. Erin's shoulders shook.

Something warm touched her arm and she jumped. Dalton squeezed and she rolled into the familiar comfort of his embrace. She forgot the imminent doom of the men on the helicopter lurking just a few yards from where she wept in her husband's arms. He let her go after a few minutes, rubbed her shoulders briskly and drew back.

"We have to go," he said.

She nodded and sniffed. "Will they think we're dead?"

"Here's hoping. Will your kayak hold two?"

"No. We'd swamp in rough water."

"Then we go on foot."

"Where?"

"As far from here as possible."

She nodded and then looked around.

"They're gone?" she asked.

"For now."

Under the cover of the trees it seemed that night had already fallen, until you glanced at the purple sky visible through the gaps in the foliage.

Where was Brian?

"Do you think they'll catch him?" Erin could not keep the tears from coming as she spoke. "I had to get him to shore. I couldn't…he couldn't…"

Dalton gathered her in.

"It was the right choice. The boy has a better chance away from us."

"I was afraid he'd upend and drown. I told him to hide and then how to walk out, but he's bleeding and scared."

"He's young and strong." Dalton released her. "He'll make it."

Was he just telling her what she needed to hear? She didn't know, but if Brian survived, it was because Dalton did as she asked. His remaining at her request had saved the boy, at least. Or it might have.

"Which way?" he asked.

"Well," she said, adjusting her pack. "We should head downriver. That's the closest place to find help."

"Then they'll expect us to head that way." Dalton looked in the opposite direction. "What's upriver?"

"Brian, I hope, and the dead."

He turned back to her, and she knew that the tears still rolled down her damp cheeks.

"I'm sorry about them, Erin. If we are lucky and smart, you'll have time to process this and grieve. But right now we must get clear of this spot. We need full cover, and the more difficult it is to follow us the better."

"Maybe we should head west awhile. There isn't much in that direction. Not a destination. Then we can turn either to Indian Lake or Lake Abanakee. There are vacation cottages on both. Golf courses, some camping." She turned in a full circle tapping her index finger on the small indentation between her upper lip and nose.

"What?" he asked.

"You know, they'll expect us on this shore."

"Because they saw my gear on the jam."

"Yes, so what if we cross the river?"

He frowned, really not wanting to get back into that sucking vortex of death.

"How?" he asked.

"I'll cross with the towrope tied to my kayak. You keep hold of the throw ball until I'm ashore. Then, you can haul back my kayak and use it to follow me."

"What if it tips on the way back? Then you're over there and I'm over here."

"Won't matter if it tips. It won't sink."

"Then we go together."

"The kayak won't sink, but it will be floating beneath the surface. We'll be swept out."

He nodded. "All right. One at a time. You first."

She gave him an impatient smirk for repeating her plan back to her, only this time taking credit, and then gave him a thumbs-up.

"Good plan. Let's do it your way."

He flushed as she sat to wait out their pursuers. The chopper continued to circle them like a shark smelling blood. Finally, their pursuers flew up and out of sight. Erin and Dalton waited for full dark so their crossing would not be noted.

Then she tumped the kayak, carrying it upside down on her head over the stretch they could not paddle. Dalton tried to take it, but the pain of stretching his arms too far above his head made it impossible. Erin carried the craft a quarter mile downriver to a spot beyond the turn. After that, he helped load her pack and held on to the thin cordage as she pushed off and flew out of his sight. He marked her progress by the line that slipped over his palms. He eyed the diminishing line, worrying that she would not reach the opposite shore before he reached the end of the towline. He wasn't sure that she'd calculated how far downriver the current would carry her before she could reach the opposite bank.

Abruptly, the towline stilled, then shuddered and moved two measured feet along. She was snagged or across. He counted the time in the rapid rasp of his breath and the sweat that rolled periodically down his back. Finally, he felt the four short tugs that signaled him to retrieve the kayak.

Dragging the craft back to him was not as easy as he had anticipated, and he was sweating and cursing by the time he sighted her kayak.

He took a moment to catch his breath and check the two vials he carried in their custom pack. Both they and the thumb drive were intact and dry. He zipped closed the case, returning it to his side pocket. Then he checked his personal weapon.

"Ready or not," he said, and climbed into the kayak, where he shimmied until the bottom cleared the bank and the river took him. Moving fast and paddling hard. The water seemed a glittering deadly ribbon. He could not see the rocks that jutted from the churning surface until they flashed past him. One pounded the underside of the kayak, making it buck like a bronco. He continued on, realizing that he was riding lower and lower in the water with each passing second. The kayak's bottom was compromised. He was certain.

The hollow core of the craft was filling with water. In other words, he was sinking.

Chapter Six

Erin's damp skin turned icy as she watched the dark shape of her kayak sinking below the surface. She caught a glimpse of the paddle sweeping before the craft and held her breath. Her husband was in the river, swimming for his life.

She grabbed her pack and cursed. It was a stupid dangerous idea to have him try to cross the river alone and at night. She knew this section and the location of the rocks that loomed from the water. Dalton did not and, as far as she knew, he had never kayaked before.

Brush and brambles lined the bank, but she raced along, searching for his head bobbing in the dark water.

"He's a strong swimmer," she told the night, but he wasn't. He was only average, his muscle mass making him what she called "a sinker."

And he should be at home on medical leave recovering from the abdominal surgery that followed the bullet wound.

She tripped, sprawled and righted herself.

"Dalton!" she shouted.

Where was he? The kayak had vanished and her paddle had been carried off. She judged the river's flow and imagined a line from where he went into the Hudson to where he might be.

He'd had loads of time in the pool and the ocean practicing escapes from crafts. He had jumped out of helicopters in to the ocean. So he'd know not to fight the river. The only thing to do was to use the forward momentum and patiently angle your stroke toward the shore.

How far would the river take him?

Her heart walloped against her ribs as she raced around tree trunks and scrambled over rocks.

What if he hit his head? What if he were unconscious?

She'd wanted a break, a time to think and a time for him to hear her fears. She didn't want him dead. That was why she'd called for a separation. He didn't see what he was doing, how dangerously he lived. And he didn't understand how his decisions affected her. If he died, oh, what if he was drowning right now?

He could be pinned against a rock or held down under a snag that wasn't even visible from above. Had he left her, finally, once and for all?

Something was moving up ahead.

Erin ran, howling like a wolf who had lost her

pack, crying his name and wailing like a banshee. Her legs pumped. When had she dropped her pack?

Was it him? Had the Fates brought him back to her once more?

I swear, I'll never leave him again. Just don't let him die. Please, please, dear Lord.

It was big, crawling up the bank. A man. Sweet Lord, it was her man.

"Dalton!"

He turned his head—lifted a hand in greeting— and collapsed on the bank.

The roar of the river blocked any reply, but he'd seen her. She fell on her hands and knees before him. Gathering him up in her arms. Rocking and weeping and babbling.

He patted her upper arm, gasping but reassuring her with his action. It only made her weep harder. He shouldn't even be here. He could have died.

It would have been her fault. He was here because of her. He'd tried the river because of her, and he'd nearly drowned…because of her.

Dalton struggled to a seat on the muddy bank. His skin was as cool as river water and his clothing drenched. It didn't have to be that cold for someone to die from exposure. Being wet upped the chances. And being weakened from exertion and the healing wounds all made him more susceptible.

She needed her pack.

"Can you stand?" she asked.

He struggled to his knees and then to his feet,

leaning heavily on her. The amount of weight that pressed down upon her nearly buckled her knees and terrified her further because he wouldn't lean so heavily if he didn't have to.

The sound of the river changed. There was a rhythmic quality that lifted to her consciousness and caused her to look skyward. A field of stars littered the velvety black and then, from upriver, came a cone of light.

"Helicopter," she said.

Dalton straightened and glanced up. "Cover," he said, and struggled up the bank. The tree line loomed like a dark curtain, impossibly far. They lumbered along, he the bear, she the fox. Nearly there when the helicopter shot past them.

The searchlight swept back and forth across the river's surface.

"They're on the logjam," he said, his voice shaking with the rest of him.

The chopper hovered, the beam shining on something beyond their line of sight.

"My kayak or my pack," he guessed.

"They'll think we drowned."

"Maybe."

"I don't understand. Why would they come after us? They must have found what they were looking for by now."

Dalton said nothing, just sank to his knees on the cushiony loam of pine needles.

"Where is your pack?" he asked.

"I dropped it."

He lifted his head and stared at her, his eyes glittering.

"In the open?"

"I'm not sure."

"Go get it, Erin. Hurry. Take cover if they go over again. Find it if you can."

"What about you?"

"I'll be here."

She stood, indecision fixing her to the spot. Go? Stay?

"We need that gear," he said.

They did.

"And if they spot it…"

Erin set off again as the helicopter continued to hover. She didn't look back as she returned to the shore and hurried upriver. She couldn't see more than a few feet before her. It would be easy to miss a green pack, but the frame, it was aluminum. She'd come too far, she thought. Must have missed it. She must have been carrying it here.

And then, finally and at last, she caught the glint of her silver water bottle.

She dashed the remaining distance and scooped up her pack. Then she turned to see the helicopter descending low on the river. Was it in the same place?

No, it was moving, shining its light on the opposite bank. The ruse was working. Still she hurried under cover and waited as it surged past her position. Then she retraced her steps.

"Dalton?"

She wasn't sure how far she needed to go, but this seemed the right distance.

"Dalton?"

"Here!"

She followed the direction of his call and found him sitting against a large tree trunk, arms wrapped about his middle. He wasn't shivering. Instead of taking that as a positive change, she saw it for what it was. When the body was cold and stopped shivering, it was dying.

Erin tore the lower boughs from the pines and set them beside the log. Then she unrolled her black foam mat and shook out her sleeping bag because the down filling needed to trap dead air within the baffles in order to insulate and help hold body heat.

When she finished, she helped him rise. He staggered and fell and then crawled as she urged him on, whispering commands like a hoarse drill sergeant. She stripped him out of his jacket, shoulder holster and personal weapon, then she tugged off the wet T-shirt and cargo pants that were predictably heavy and likely carrying his service weapon and extra clips for his pistol. All were wet, but that was a problem for another time.

"I'm not cold," he whispered, his words slurring.

He stretched out in the open sleeping bag and lay on both the mat and pine boughs. She zipped him in.

Erin thought about calling the emergency number of the Department of Environmental Conservation.

The rangers could call the New York State Police Aviation Unit or the Eagle Valley Search Dogs, but she very much feared that rescue would be hours away. So she left her phone off and stowed for the time being. Right now she needed shelter and to get Dalton warm.

She was a survival expert and knew the rule of threes. The body could survive three minutes without air, three hours without shelter, less depending on the weather and their physical condition, three days without water and three weeks without food.

She fitted her pack half under the log at his head and then set to work on the shelter. Fallen sticks and branches littered the forest floor and she gathered them by the armful, making a great pile. Then she constructed a brush shelter around him using the log beside which he lay as the center beam and leaning the larger sticks against it. It was low to the ground, easy to miss if you were not looking. She did not know if the men who had killed her party would follow them into the woods, but she was taking no chances.

Her tent was too geometrical and too light to make good cover. But her camo tarp could work if she used it correctly. Erin laid the ten-by-ten tarp over the logs and sticks, then staked it down on the opposite side of the downed trunk. The remaining four feet she stretched out away from the log before securing it to the ground. Then she added evergreen boughs to further disguise their burrow.

Erin stepped back to study the structure she had built. The resulting shelter was roughly the shape of a lean-to and stood only two feet tall at the highest point, tapering to the ground from there and was no taller than the fallen tree trunk. The tarp would break the cold wind that was rising carrying the scent of rain.

As the helicopter searched the far bank, she finished all but the small gap needed to crawl inside. This she would close once she was beside her husband. The fact that Dalton did not move to help her frightened her greatly.

Shivering herself, exhausted and sick at heart, Erin crawled in next to Dalton. Before she closed the opening, she watched as the helicopter hovered beyond the barrier of tree trunks and crossed the glistening water. That too was a problem for another time. They could no longer run. So, it was time to hide.

Erin wiggled in beside her husband. His skin was cold as marble. She managed to get the zipper up and around them. The bag was designed for one, but accommodated them both with Dalton on his back and her tucked against him on her side. She knew how much body heat was lost from the top of a person's head so she tugged at the drawstring, bringing the top of the bag down around Dalton's head like the hood of a parka.

Still at last, she pressed her warm body to his icy one. Gradually, her temperature dropped and she shivered. Dalton lay unmoving except for the shallow rise and fall of his chest.

What if he was bleeding inside again?

She could do nothing if he was, and that was why her mind fixed upon it. Why was that?

When one shoulder began to ache, she pushed herself on top of Dalton. She inhaled fresh pine, damp earth and the aftershave that still lingered faintly on Dalton's skin. He lifted an arm across her back, holding her in his sleep. His movement made her tear up. By the time she shifted to his opposite side, he was shivering.

The helicopter rotors continued to spin and the beam of light crossed over them twice. She wasn't sure when the chopper finally moved off. Sometime after Dalton had stopped shivering.

She fell asleep with the uneasy feeling that the men who had murdered her party had not given up. A cold wind rushed through the shelter, cooling her face. She tasted rain.

Sometime later, the storm struck, hitting the tree canopy first, rousing Erin from uneasy slumber. Dalton's breathing had changed to a slow, steady draw and his heart beat in a normal rhythm. Eventually the rain penetrated the interlocking branches of the trees and the droplets pattered on the dry leaves. The torrent of water grew in volume until she could no longer hear the river rush.

The sky lit in a brilliant flash of white and Erin began her counting as she waited for the thunder.

She didn't like being under the trees in such a storm. Tall trees were natural lightning rods, and the wind could bring down limbs and dead trees on hapless campers. It was why she had selected the fateful rocky outcropping.

She imagined the rain merging with the drying blood on the bodies of the ones she had left behind, and her chest constricted.

"Erin?" Dalton whispered.

"Yes?"

"You okay?"

"I don't think so."

"The chopper gone?"

"Yes."

"I thought I just saw the spotlight."

The thunder rolled over and through them.

"It's the storm."

He relaxed back into their nest. "Good. Make it harder to track us."

"Why would they want to track us?" she asked, and in answer heard his gentle snore.

Erin rolled to her side, pressing her back against him and curling her arms before herself. The thunder was still a mile off, but over the next quarter hour it passed overhead.

The cascade of water finally penetrated their burrow, soaking the evergreen and running down the needles and tarp away from where they rested.

Gradually the rainfall diminished, and the sound of the river returned, rushing endlessly. When she next roused it was to some unfamiliar sound. She stiffened, listening. The gray gloom inside their nest told her that morning approached. She could now see the sides of the shelter above her.

The sound came again, this time recognizable. It was the snapping of a stick underneath the foot of something moving close at hand.

Chapter Seven

Erin strained to listen to the creature moving close to their shelter. Squirrel or possum, maybe. Or a deer, perhaps. When animals moved, they sounded much larger than they actually were. She'd seen grown men startle in terror from the crackle of dried leaves under the paws of a scurrying chipmunk.

The sound came again. That was no chipmunk.

Now there was another snap of a branch, this time coming from a slightly different direction. Dalton's eyes popped open and she pressed a hand over his mouth. Whatever was out there, she did not want to reveal their position.

DALTON WOKE WITH a jolt to feel Erin's warm hand pressed across his mouth. He shifted only his eyes to look at her. In the gray predawn gloom, he could see little. But his body was on high alert.

She had heard it, too. He was certain from the stiffness of her body and the way she cocked her head to one side, listening. Something was coming. To him it sounded like the even tread of boots. He had been on enough covert ops to recognize the sound of a line of men moving in sequence.

He lifted his head from the sleeping bag. Listening.

Where was his gun?

The sound came from the right and left. He counted the footfalls. He heard three distinct individuals moving together, searching, he guessed, the forest on this side of the river.

Had they already finished their sweep of the opposite bank?

Where the hell was his gun?

The group continued forward and then passed them. Why hadn't they seen them?

Dalton gazed up at the unfamiliar roof some eight inches above his head. They were in some sort of shelter constructed of broken sticks leaning on a large fallen log and then covered with a camo tarp. More branches on the outside, judging from the way the light cut through the tarp. His gaze swept above his head and down to his toes. Then he turned his face so that his lips pressed to his wife's ear.

"They missed us."

Now she turned her head to whisper into his ear.

"What if they come back?"

He did not answer. But he knew exactly. It was not to tie up loose ends or to silence them forever. It was to retrieve what had been stolen from them or from their employers. They were acting on orders to retrieve the contents of the red nylon cooler. Just as the pilot had told them. These men would keep coming until they recovered what he carried. And he would stop at nothing to get it into the hands of his own government.

But first he had to empty his bladder.

Erin was still for a very long time. Finally, she shifted beside him, lifting her knee across his thigh, rising up to one elbow to stare down at him.

"They were searching along this side of the river."

"Yes."

"Should we stay here or make a run for it?"

"I've got to get up. Let me do a little recon."

"Good plan, except you're naked, your clothes are wet, your gun is wet and recon means leaving me alone. Let me rephrase that. Bad plan. Really, really bad."

"I still have to get up."

"Me, too."

"After you then. I haven't climbed out of a fox-hole in some time."

"It's a brush shelter."

Erin removed the sticks that obscured the opening. Then she wiggled out of the bag to crouch beside the tree. She saw immediately why they were invisible to their pursuers. Several more pine boughs had fallen during the storm. Her shelter seemed just more debris.

Not only that, the warm ground in the cool air had resulted in a low mist that crept around the tree trunks and hugged the earth. To disappear, one only had to lie flat.

She took her time listening and looking for the men. Seeing nothing, she called back to Dalton and then moved away to relieve herself. When she returned to him, he was crouching naked beside the shelter.

"It's freezing out here."

"The mornings can be chilly."

"I'm shriveled up like the… Do you have anything that I can wear?"

Erin moved to the shelter to slide her pack out of the gap. She sorted through her gear and retrieved the plastic rain poncho.

"Maybe this?" She offered the poncho and then added one of his olive green T-shirts.

He held the familiar garment aloft. "Why did you bring this?"

"Hey, don't read more into it than there is. It's soft and I like to sleep in it." She did not like his self-satisfied smile.

A moment later he had slipped into the T-shirt. As his head vanished into the fabric she glanced to his stomach. She always admired the heavy musculature of his chest and stomach, especially in motion. But this time her gaze tracked to the swollen red suture line at the flesh just above his hip bone. The man should be home, resting and not lifting anything over forty pounds.

Dalton tugged down on the hem of the cotton

T-shirt and then donned the poncho. He chose to wear his damp cargo pants commando style. Then he spent the next twenty minutes disassembling, cleaning and drying his pistol. He dried every bullet in the four clips that he had stowed in the pockets of his pants.

Erin occupied herself scattering the branches used for her shelter. Then she stuffed the sleeping bag back into its nylon bag, rolled her foam pad and collected the tarp. She stowed all of these but the high density foam bedroll into her pack. That she tied on the top.

"Ready?" he asked.

"Which way?" she asked.

"Away from our company. When they don't find us, they'll backtrack"

"You want me to call the forest rangers?"

"Is your phone still off?"

"How did you know it was off?"

His mouth tipped down. "I tried calling you yesterday. Kept flipping to voice mail."

"I told you I wouldn't be calling."

"You did."

Now she was scowling. "I'll keep it off for now."

Dalton removed the strap from her shoulder and took her pack.

"You shouldn't carry that," she said, staring pointedly at his middle and the healing surgical scars that she knew were there.

"Circumstances being as they are, I am."

"We still have to talk about this."

He nodded and set off. Erin knew he'd likely rather face those mercenaries than have a talk with her, and that was exactly the problem, wasn't it? But they were going to talk, and even commandos were not going to keep her from saying her piece.

If he didn't like it, that was just too darn bad. Next time maybe he'd stay home when she asked him.

By the time Dalton finally stopped, the gray dawn had morphed into a fine drizzle that coated the leaves and dripped down upon them. It saturated her hair and dampened her clothing. Erin could see from his pallor that Dalton had pushed too hard and traveled too many miles.

"Where do you think we are?" he asked.

They'd been traveling in roughly a northerly direction according to her compass, paralleling the river, and she could guess the distance at three miles of scrambling down bramble-covered ravines and up lichen-covered rock faces. The topography on this side of the river was challenging, and the closer they got to the gorges the steeper the climb would become.

"Don't you know?" she asked.

He shook his head.

"Then just maybe you should let the one with the compass and maps lead."

He pressed his lips together in that suffering look, and her internal temperature rose to a near boil. She reminded herself that he'd nearly died last month and again last night. It seemed he was determined to leave her. Her leaving was intended to keep that from happening, but somehow it had just made everything worse.

She removed the bottle from the pack she carried and offered it to him.

"Almost empty," he said, refusing.

"I can fill it anywhere. I have a filtration system on this bottle."

"You mean I've been conserving all morning for no reason?"

"No, there was a reason. You didn't ask me."

His eyes lifted skyward as if praying for patience, and then he drank all that was left in the bottle.

"Why don't we just call DEC?"

"DEC?" he asked.

"Department of Environmental Conservation. The forest rangers. They can dispatch a helicopter and lift us out of here."

"No."

"Why not?"

He shook his head and looked skyward as if expecting a phantom helicopter. Honestly, the man seemed to want to do everything the hard way.

"Dalton, why?"

"The call for air evac would be via radio, and that transmission is being monitored by our pursuers."

"You don't know that."

"It's what I would do."

"Well, then, let me at least send search and rescue after Brian Peters and to my group." Her voice broke on the last word and she clamped her mouth closed to keep from crying.

"Your mobile is still off?"

"Yes. Why?"

"If the kid made it out, then they already know what happened and where."

She thought of the teen alone on the trail and the worry squeezed at her heart. "Do you think he's safe?"

Her husband offered no assurances and his expression remained grim. "He's a wounded kid and they're trained mercenaries. He went the way you told me that they'd expect us to go."

She had sent him straight into more trouble. Erin scowled. "I never should have left him."

"If you hadn't, we'd all be dead. His only chance was away from us. You made the right call. In any case, you are overdue to check in. When DEC finds your party, they'll know you are missing with three kayaks. But if you switch on that phone our pursuers will find us."

"How?"

"Forest Rangers will request GPS coordinates from the county 911."

Erin said no more as she studied the map for several minutes. "You want to backtrack to Lake Abanakee or continue downriver to the community of North River?"

"Neither. Those are the two directions they will expect us to travel. What else have you got?"

"Why are they even following us? Is it because we are witnesses?"

Dalton's gaze shifted away. Erin scowled as she remembered something.

"You took that cooler. The one from the helicopter. I saw it in your kayak."

"The pilot entrusted the information—"

"To me! And I left it behind. I left it because our lives are more valuable to me than some flash drive and a pair of glass vials."

He saw the look in her eyes, registering what he had done. He didn't deny it. But neither did he offer reassurance. She was right. He'd put them in danger.

"But you lost all your gear with your kayak. If they were searching, they should have found both. Even if the cooler popped out of your kayak…"

"It didn't. I tied it down."

Dalton's eyes shifted back to meet hers and she saw the guilty look on his face.

"Where is it?" she demanded.

Dalton lifted his hands in a gesture meant to placate. "Now, honey. Listen to me."

"Where?"

His right hand moved to the side pocket on his cargo pants. He gave the full pocket a little pat.

"Why in the name of heaven would you risk our lives for whatever trouble that pilot was carrying?"

Dalton reached for her shoulders and she stepped

away. Then she released the waist buckle at her middle and dropped her pack. She spent the next several moments stalking back and forth like a caged animal, gathering her fury about her like a cloak. Finally, she came to a complete stop, pivoting to face him.

"You just don't get it. This is why I wanted a break. This…" She waved her hand in a circular motion and continued speaking. "This obsession with playing the hero. It's not our job to deliver that nonsense. It was his."

"This is bigger than that," said Dalton. "This could save thousands of lives. Maybe our own."

"If we don't get killed in the process." She turned her back on him and covered her face with her hands.

Tentatively, he wrapped an arm around her shoulders and turned her to face him.

"Erin, I'm sorry. But I didn't see a choice."

She shook her head. "And that's where you're wrong. There's always a choice. The choice to reenlist in the most dangerous arm of the Marines."

"I left them because you were unhappy."

"I wasn't unhappy being married to a marine. I was unhappy being married to a marine who insisted on being on the front line of every assignment."

"I quit because of you."

"You didn't quit. You just shifted from one dangerous assignment to the next. New York City Real Time Crime Center? Come on, Dalton. What is the difference between that and Vice?"

"It's not undercover work."

"You're a cop. You're a target."

"Is that what you think I am?"

"They shot you! They killed your partner."

"Not while I was on a call."

"What difference does that make? You were in a coma, Dalton. You didn't have to attend your partner's funeral. You didn't have to see them give a flag to his widow. You didn't have to comfort his children. I did that. I did that alone while you were recovering from internal injuries."

"I understand how you must feel."

"Clearly you don't or you would have stayed home as I asked. You would have considered that my fears are justified."

"And you'd be dead now."

"As opposed to in a day from now? If you really believe that those guys are after us, trained killers, what chance do we have? They have helicopters and guns. All we have is each other."

"Maybe that's enough."

She rolled her eyes. "Oh, Dalton. Just leave it. Put it on a rock on a bright red T-shirt with a note that says, 'Enjoy!' and let's get out of here with our lives."

"That's why I love you, Erin. You are a survivor."

She pressed her lips tight and glared. "The way you are headed, I'll have to be."

"Don't be like that."

"Like what? I'm trying to keep you alive. To save you from yourself because if I don't, one way or another, you're leaving me. Getting shot at, blown up in

Afghanistan, coming home with knife wounds and now carrying a vial of something that, if it breaks open in your pocket, will kill us both."

She loved him, but she was not going to stand over his coffin and accept a flag from a grateful city or nation. If you couldn't stop the oncoming train, sometimes all you could do was step out of its way.

He stared down at her with that hangdog look, and she tried and failed not to feel his sorrow.

"How do you see this ending?" she asked.

"We make it out and get this to the FBI in Albany."

"Fine." She shouldered her pack and stared up at the victorious smile on his handsome face, and she ignored the jolt of awareness that he stirred in her. "And then I want a divorce."

Chapter Eight

Erin studied the topographical map. "If we walk along the gorge beside the Boreas River, we'll run into North Woods Club Road."

"How far?"

"Roughly three miles east to the confluence of the Boreas River and Hudson, bushwhacking because there is no trail. Then it's a two-mile uphill hike, steep for the first mile or so, on a marked trail to the gravel road. From there we can head west to a small community at the terminus of the road or east to Minerva. The community looks like about five houses. Either one is somewhere around five more miles."

"Ten miles."

"Only six to the road. We can get help there."

"Or get intercepted."

"The rain will fill the rivers and make the going slippery, but we should reach the road in a couple of hours. We can call the rangers."

He looked unconvinced.

"They can search for Brian, send help, and I'll tell them not to use radio communication."

"You can't guarantee it. With so many rangers, someone will pick up a radio."

"Who do you want to call, your detective bureau?"

"Too far. But I could have them call for help once we get out of the woods."

"What about my camp director? He can drive to the station. By now they've found—" she struggled to swallow "—my group. He'll believe me when I tell him we are on the run, being stalked. And if Brian got through, they'll know our situation. We know there's help out there. We just have to get to them or help them find us."

"When we get closer to the road."

"Fine." She kept hold of her pack and the map, leading the way back. "You know, there will be rafting groups on the river all day. We might get one of them to pick us up."

"No. They'll be at the terminus of every rafting trip."

"How many of these people do you really think there are?"

"Three in the chopper last night and three in the woods beside our shelter. Plus, the ones who shot the chopper down."

"They might be the same group."

"I don't know how many. Neither do you. So assume everyone we meet is one of them."

She'd seen what they could do, and she did not question her husband's assessment of their situation.

Erin led the way, using her compass only and staying well away from the Hudson. She stopped to fill the water bottle at a spring. All she had were several power bars she kept for emergencies, which this surely was. She handed Dalton the lemon zest bar and kept the chocolate chip for herself. She peeled back the wrapping and glanced up to see the second and last bite of the lemon zest disappear into Dalton's mouth.

"When did you last eat?" she asked.

"Yesterday morning."

He was a big man and burned a lot more calories than she did. She rummaged in her pack and offered a second bar.

"You have more?" His brows lifted in that adorable way that made her want to kiss his face.

"Yes, plenty." Plenty being one.

Midmorning, they paused at a stream and Dalton returned her poncho. He did fill out the shirt she slept in, and she surreptitiously enjoyed the view of his biceps bulging as he lifted the bottle to his lips and drank. The sight made her own mouth go dry.

Erin glanced away, but too late. She was already remembering him naked beneath her last night. Dalton's large, strong body never failed to arouse her. It was just his attitude that pushed her aside. Just once she'd like to have him choose them above protecting the city or the nation or whatever it was he thought he was doing. If he was right, the men hunting them were still out there.

Despite her reservations, her mind swept back to the last time they'd made love. Before the shooter had walked up to her husband's unmarked police unit and shot his partner, Chris Wirimer, in the head before turning the pistol on Dalton. The shooter had targeted the pair solely because they wore police dress uniforms. They were en route to attend the annual medal day ceremony in Lower Manhattan. The gunman had managed to get a bullet between the front and back of Dylan's body armor. It had taken six hours to patch all the bleeders from the bullet, which had traveled between his body armor and his hip bone from front to back stopping only when it had reached the back panel of his flak jacket. A through and through with no internal organ damage, but Dalton had nearly bled out, nearly left her in the way she always feared he would.

From beneath the cover of the canopy of hardwood and pine, Erin again heard the rush of running water. A short time later they reached the Doreas River, flowing fast and swollen from the heavy rains. Here at the river's terminus, the water stretched forty feet from side to side. Erin knew that farther up, the river ran through narrow gorges on the stretch of white water known as Guts and Glory. Here, it tumbled and frothed, making for an excellent run.

She found the trail easily and turned north. Looking back, she could see where the two rivers met. She did not linger as she led them up the steep, muddy trail. Dalton's breathing was labored, and she paused to let him rest. She didn't like his grayish color and was angry again that he'd decided to ambush her instead of giving himself time to heal and her time to think.

She turned her head at the jangle of a dog's collar. A few moments later a young black Labrador retriever appeared wearing a red nylon collar and no leash. Its pink tongue lolled and it paused for just a moment upon sighting Erin, then dashed forward in jubilant excitement.

Erin laughed and offered her hand. The dog wore a harness and was likely carrying her own food and water. Erin stooped to give the dog a scratch behind the ears. She glanced at her collar, fingering the vaccination tag and the ID.

"Jet, huh?" she asked.

The dog half closed her eyes and sat at her feet.

Erin glanced up the trail, waiting for the dog's owner to appear. She did, a few moments later—a fit older woman with braided graying hair who wore a slouch hat that covered most of her face, hiking shorts and a T-shirt, cotton button-up shirt, wool socks and worn hiking boots. In her hands she carried a hiking stick, and there was a day pack upon her back.

"Oh, hello," said the woman, drawing to a halt. "He's friendly."

Erin wrinkled her nose because the dog was

clearly female. That was odd. There was something not right about that woman. Erin took a reflexive step back, trying to determine why her skin was tingling a warning.

"You been to the Hudson?" asked the woman.

The dog did not dart back to her master but instead sat beside Erin. A chill crept over her. She took another step away.

"Yes, it's only a mile and a half down this trail."

"You camping along here?" asked the woman.

"Yes."

"You alone?" the woman asked.

Alone?

Erin turned back in the direction they had come and was surprised to see only the dog at her side. Where was Dalton? Erin's skin prickled as if she had rolled in a patch of nettles. She turned back to face this new threat.

"Yes, why?" Erin thought the woman's smile looked forced and she realized the hiker was younger than she appeared. She wondered vaguely if the gray braided hair was actually attached to this woman's head.

"Where's your partner?"

"What partner?" Erin asked.

"Detective Dalton Stevens." The female drew a small handgun from her pocket and pointed it at Erin's belly.

Erin's mouth dropped open and her heart seemed

to pulse in the center of her throat. She could not have spoken if she had tried.

"Does he have it? Or do you?"

"I don't know what you're talking about."

The woman snorted. "Yes, you do. Drop the pack."

Erin did as she was told.

The woman waved Erin back with the barrel of the pistol. Then she moved forward, keeping her gun on Erin as she swept the surroundings with a gaze.

"Come out, Detective, or I shoot your wife."

Chapter Nine

Erin faced the female pointing a pistol at her belly, clearing her throat before she spoke.

"Is this your dog?" Erin asked.

The woman's mouth quirked. "Took it off a pair that were camping back a ways. Unfortunately for them, I'm not so good with faces and I thought they were you. Should have checked before I shot them in their sleeping bags. Lesson learned."

Erin couldn't keep from covering her mouth with one hand.

"Don't figure they need a dog anymore and I thought it added to the whole look." She glanced at the trees on either side of the path. Then she raised her voice. "Detective? I'm counting to three. One…"

Erin jumped at the report of the pistol. Her hands went to her middle, but she felt no pain. Before her, her attacker sank to her knees. Dalton stepped from cover. Pistol aimed and cradled between his two hands as he moved forward with feline grace.

Her canine companion moved forward to greet

him, but Dalton ignored the dog, focusing all his attention on the woman, who had released her pistol and sunk to her side. Blood bloomed on the front of her T-shirt and frothed from her mouth.

"How many are you?" asked Dalton.

She laughed, sending frothy pink droplets of blood dribbling down her chin.

"We're like ants at a picnic."

Dalton knelt beside her, transferring the gun to one hand; with the other he patted her down. His search yielded a second pistol, car keys, phone and several strips of plastic zip ties. Erin's stomach twisted at the thought of what she had intended to do with these.

She crept forward and removed the floppy blue hat. The gray braid fell away with the headgear. The end of the braid was secured with a hair tie to the hat's interior tag and looked to have been sliced from someone's head.

Had she stolen a woman's dog, hair and walking stick along with her life? Erin glanced at the plaid shirt and noted it was miles too big. Somewhere up ahead were the victims of this woman's attack. Erin feared she might be sick.

Dalton pocketed the key, one of the pistols, radio, phone and a folding knife. He extended the second gun to Erin.

"Take it."

She did, hoping it would not go off in her pocket.

"Who are you?" Dalton asked the downed woman.

"One of Siming's Army."

"Who?"

"You'll find out." Her smile was a ghastly sight with her lips painted red with her own blood. "The first Deathbringer. You have it. We'll get it back."

"Deathbringer," whispered Erin remembering the name.

The woman turned to look at her. "Oh! So you know them. Very good. One. Two. Three. Each body to his own fate."

The woman began to choke on her blood, struggling to draw air into her damaged lungs. Erin glanced at Dalton, who shook his head. She didn't need him to tell her that the woman was dying.

"Why are you doing this?" asked Erin, her voice angry now.

"A corrupt system must fall."

"You murdered hikers because of a corrupt system? That's insane."

"Acceptable—" she gasped and gurgled "—losses."

"We need to get off the trail," said Dalton.

He stood and Erin followed, hesitating.

"We just leave her?"

He nodded and offered his hand. "Come on. Off the trail."

The dog danced along beside them, and no amount of shooing would send her away.

"We'll have to take her," said Erin.

Dalton shook his head, adjusting the grip on the gun still in his hand.

"You will not shoot a dog!" she said, stepping between him and the black Lab.

Dalton smiled. "I was just going to tie her up on the trail."

"I'll do it." Which she did, but she also filled the water dish she carried in her pack and fed her dry food. When she left Jet, tied with a bit of her sash cord in plain view of anyone who came along here, she imagined the reaction of the poor next hiker who would stumble on this turn in the trail.

Then she petted the dog's soft, warm head and said goodbye.

When she returned, it was to find Dalton watching her.

"We should get a dog," he said.

Erin sighed and lifted her pack. "I don't like leaving her."

"We'll send somebody for her when we're safe. She'll be okay until then."

They bushwhacked uphill, staying well away from the trail and stopping when they heard people moving in their direction.

Dalton squatted beside her as they waited for the group to pass.

When he spoke, his voice was a whisper. "Once they report that death, Siming's Army will know our position. We need to move faster."

"Well, I lost my kayak."

They hurried up the rest of the slope, pausing

only when they heard something tearing uphill in their direction.

Dalton motioned her to take cover and ducked behind a tree trunk. Then he drew his handgun, aiming it toward the disturbance. Something was running full out right at them.

She watched Dalton sight down the barrel of his gun, gaze focused and expression intent. She knew he would protect her and she knew he loved her. It should be enough. But who was protecting him?

The barrel of his pistol dropped and he relaxed his arms, his aim shifting to the ground. She saw him slide the safety home as he straightened.

"I don't believe this." Dalton stepped from cover.

Erin glanced around the tree trunk to see a streak of black fur barreling toward them.

"Jet!" she said.

The Lab leaped to her thighs, tail wagging merrily. Then the canine greeted Dalton by racing the few steps that separated them before throwing herself to the ground to twist back and forth in the dead leaves, paws waving and tail thumping.

Dalton holstered his pistol in the waistband of his pants and stooped to pet the dog's ribs. This caused Jet to spring to her feet to explore the area.

"She doesn't seem very broken up by the death of her owners," said Erin.

"Because she's decided we're her owners."

Erin grabbed Jet when she made her next pass.

She sat before Erin, gazing up adoringly, her pink tongue lolling.

"She chewed through the sash cord." Erin held up the frayed evidence of her deduction. "She'll have to come with us."

"Not a great idea."

"I'm not leaving her again."

"She could give away our position."

She placed a fist on one hip. "If you can carry a deadly virus, I'm allowed a dog."

He twisted his mouth in frustration and then blew out of his nostrils.

"Fine. But let's go."

They scrambled over roots and waded through ferns that brushed her knees. She walked parallel to the trail that led to the gravel road, far enough away so as not to be seen. This made for slow going, and there were two places where they had to scramble up large sections of gray rock.

Mercifully, they did not see the couple that their attacker had mentioned before they finally reached the road. Dalton grasped her arm before she left the cover of the woods. Erin hunched down as he glanced right and left.

"Now we need to find the parking area for that trail. Good chance they might be there."

"We could call 911 with that woman's phone. If they're tracking her GPS signal, it'll just confirm she's where she's supposed to be—looking for us."

"Maybe. You know where the parking area is?"

"Usually right beside the trailhead. Sometimes across the road. That would be that way." She pointed to her right.

"Stay in the woods."

They picked their way over downed trees and through last year's fallen leaves, making a racket that Erin feared could be heard for miles. Under the cover of the pines, the ground was soft and their tread quiet. Jet found a stick which she tried unsuccessfully to get Dalton to throw.

Erin was willing and Jet dashed back and forth joyfully engaged in the game of fetch. Dalton came to a halt and Erin pulled up beside him. Through the maze of pine trunks she caught the glint of sunlight on metal. Automobiles. They had reached the lot.

She took hold of the dog's collar as Dalton scouted ahead. In a few minutes he returned, holding the key fob.

"This doesn't unlock either of the cars in that lot."

"What does that mean?"

"It means she was dropped at the trailhead, which means they are close."

Erin absently stroked the dog as she stared out at the lot. "What do you recommend?"

"Use her phone. Call the state police and wait for them behind cover."

They crossed into the open and then jogged across the mowed grass and over the gravel road to the opposite side. From a place in deep cover that still afforded a glimpse of the road, Dalton made his 911 call and was connected to NY State Police dispatch.

"I'm calling because my wife is on a kayaking expedition." Dalton gave the name of her camp and said that he had not heard from her. He flipped the phone to speaker so Erin could also hear the dispatcher.

"Yes, we have them listed as overdue. DEC rangers are searching."

"Should I be worried?"

"I can report that they located their camp from last night. No signs of trouble."

Erin scowled and opened her mouth to speak. Dalton held her gaze and shook his head.

"Whereabouts was that?"

There was a pause, and then the dispatcher correctly mentioned the bluff over the Hudson where her group had been murdered.

"I'll check back. Thank you." Dalton disconnected.

"What about the bodies? The helicopter piece that killed Carol? The tents, kayaks? What about the blood, Dalton?"

He gripped the phone in his hand. "The storm would have washed away the blood. Most of the helicopter sank in the Hudson, and as for the rest, someone had to remove all the evidence of the massacre."

"Just how darn big is Siming's Army?" she asked.

Chapter Ten

"Call your camp director," said Dalton.

He passed her the phone and she placed the call. Erin gripped the phone in both hands as she held it out and on Speaker. The call was answered on the first ring. Her director, Oscar Boyle, a sweet, fortyish guy with tons of canoeing experience and a sunny disposition, picked up the call. Today, however, his voice relayed an unfamiliar note of anxiety.

"Erin! Oh, thank goodness. We've been going crazy. Your husband is here. He wants to speak to you."

"My husband?" She glanced at Dalton.

"Yes. He showed up yesterday to surprise you but couldn't locate your camp, so he… Do you want to speak to him? Wait, tell me where you guys are. Did you move camp because of the storm?"

Dalton gave her the cut sign and she ended the call. Then she handed back the phone.

"Do you think they'll have our coordinates?"

"Not yet. Your director will have to ask 911 to

check this call and the coordinates. But they'll get around to it and they'll have this phone number, the registered owner, that is *if* it's not a burner, and after that, our position. We have to move." Dalton retrieved the phone and flicked it off.

"Which way?"

"They'll expect us to use the road and head toward Minerva. So either we go back into the woods in a direction they can't predict, or we walk on the road toward the fish and game club."

"Why there?"

"Food, shelter and possibly weapons."

"We need to get rid of that package. Just leave it on top of a car with the thumb drive. They find it and they'll stop chasing us."

He gave her a long look and she set her jaw.

"Is that really what you want me to do?"

She paced back and forth, and Jet crouched and leaped, trying to get Erin to throw the stick that the dog had carried across the road with her.

Erin stooped and took possession of the stick. Then she threw it with all her might. Jet tore off after it, of course. Erin turned to face Dalton.

"No, damn it, I don't."

He smiled. "That's my girl."

She rubbed her forehead. "We could hike over that mountain and come down at the town of Minerva. Or we could head west, past the gun club toward Lake Abanakee. Or we could backtrack to the Hudson."

"Distances?"

"Maybe twenty miles to the lake. Five up and over the mountain to Minerva, and that's if we use the trail system."

"Maybe Minerva," he said, but his face was grim and she could feel the tension in him.

He didn't like their chances. She knew that frown, the deep lines that cut across his brow.

"They're getting closer, aren't they?" she asked.

He met her gaze and told her the truth. "Yes."

"And you think this is worth the risk of our lives?" she asked.

He glanced away. "It's worth the risk to my life." His gaze flashed back to her. "But not the risk to yours."

She swallowed down the lump, her throat emitting a squeaking sound.

"I have another idea," she said, and explained it to him. She knew there was an old trestle bridge that could take them safely across the Hudson and, from there, it was an easy eight-mile hike to the community of North River. "I don't think they'll be expecting us in the river now."

He nodded. "Yeah, that might work."

Was it the best plan? She didn't know. Dalton used their attacker's phone once more to call one of his comrades. Henry Larson had been in Dalton's unit for five years and they had come up through the academy together. He gave Henry, now in Queens, NY, their basic location and where they expected to be this evening. Henry would be calling the FBI the minute Dalton hung up. With luck they'd have help they could trust in about seven hours.

Dalton left the phone behind.

The walk downhill, off the trail, took most of the afternoon. She hoped they could reach the trestle bridge after the last group passed by. The rafters on this section were not looking for the kind of jarring thrills of the paddlers who shot the canyon. This trip was more family friendly. She had to be certain they crossed the bridge without any raft expedition or kayakers spotting them.

They paused just off the abandoned railroad bridge, behind cover and looked upriver. Erin had never crossed such a bridge and worried about the wide gaps between the horizontal wooden slats beneath the twin rails.

"What about the dog?" she asked. "Will she be able to cross the trestle bridge?"

"We'll see."

Erin heard the group before seeing them, their shouts as they descended one of the gentler falls. Dalton and Erin held Jet, remaining in hiding as the rafters floated by one after another. Only when they were out of sight did they stand.

"How deep is it here?" he asked.

"Deep enough to jump. I've seen teenagers do it."

Dalton looked over and down to the river some forty feet below. "Seems a great way to win a Darwin Award."

He spoke of the online list of folks who had,

through acts of extreme stupidity, removed themselves from the gene pool by accidentally killing themselves.

He looked to her. "You ever try it?"

"I only like heights when I'm strapped into a belay system."

Dalton studied the river. "There might be lookouts."

"It's the only way across without swimming."

"Yes, that's what worries me. Ready?"

She nodded and started across. Jet whined and danced back and forth, anxious about following.

Erin turned back and called to the dog. Jet took a tentative step. Then another. The dog leaped from one slat to the next, jumping the eighteen-inch gaps. Dalton continued along, ignoring their four-legged companion and passing Erin.

Erin followed but then turned back in time to see Jet miss landing with her back feet, scrabble with her front and vanish between the slats. The splash came a moment later.

She glanced at Dalton, who was already kneeling, hands on the rail, as he judged his target and the distance down.

Erin ditched her pack, acting faster than Dalton.

"What are you doing?" he asked, standing now, reaching. She returned his frown and then jumped into the river after Jet. She heard his shout on the way down.

"Erin!"

The current was swift, even here on the wide-open section of the Hudson. She pulled and kicked, lifting her head only to mark the location of her new best friend. Jet paddled toward her, of course, instead of using the current, but the river swept her away. Erin swam harder, grabbing the dog's collar before turning toward the opposite bank.

Above, Dalton jogged along, carrying her pack, following her with an intent frown on his face.

She struggled against the current, using a scissor kick and one arm. Jet thrashed at the water, managing to keep her head up as they inched toward the southern bank. They made land at the same time as Dalton disappeared into the tree line above.

Racing, he reached her in record time.

"That was stupid," said Dalton.

She wiggled her brows.

Jet shook off the water, tail wagging as the dog immediately began sniffing the ground about them. Then she waded back into the river.

"Jet, come!" she shouted.

"You are not diving in after her again," said Dalton.

"No need."

Jet dashed back to her, tongue lolling and eyes half-closed.

"Someone will sleep well tonight," she said. When she turned her attention from Jet to Dalton, it was to see him scowling at her with both hands on his hips.

"You could have died," he said.

"Yes? How does that make you feel?" she asked.

"Mad as hell."

"Well, now you know how I feel every darn day."

His scowl deepened, sending wide furrows across his forehead.

"So it's all right to risk your neck for a dog but not for the safety of a nation?"

She lifted her chin, ready for the fight he obviously wanted. "I jumped to keep *you* from jumping."

"I wasn't…" He stopped just short of lying.

Erin shouldered her pack and turned to go and Jet followed. Dalton had caught up before they reached the highway.

"Do you think anyone saw us cross?" she asked.

"I don't know, but if there was anyone spotting, they couldn't have missed you and that darn dog."

Chapter Eleven

Erin changed into dry clothing and they ate the last of her food stores. Then they endured another four-mile hike over relatively flat terrain on the railroad tracks that flanked the river. Their trip was stalled twice by hikers and once by horseback riders. Thankfully, most travel in this area was by river rather than by land. Still, Erin was wistful as she watched the young women riding slowly past on a buckskin and a small chestnut mare. Her tired legs made it especially hard not to bum a lift.

She got her bearings when they reached the garnet processing plant, where abrasives were produced from the crushed red garnets mined nearby. She'd been on the mine tour more than once and knew the working mine was south of North Creek.

When they reached Route 28, Erin's ankles and knees pulsed with her heart, and her pack seemed exponentially heavier. Dalton drew to a halt and Jet groaned, then lay down, panting.

"You have anything we can pawn or trade for a

hotel room?" Dalton asked, studying the mine plant from behind cover. "And maybe dinner?"

"No, but I do have three hundred dollars in my wallet. You lose your wallet?"

"I only have fifty bucks left," he admitted.

"Always prepared, except for things you have to pay for," she joked, and they shared a smile.

"How well do you know the area?"

"Drove through it, passed all the rafting outfits along the highway. Post office, roadhouse and bed-and-breakfast."

"Fancy. What about a motel?"

"I'm sure we could ask."

"I could. I'm traveling alone with my dog. You need to stay out of sight," he said.

"I can do that. I'll wait right here." The prospect of stopping and resting appealed.

"Let's get closer to town. That way?" he asked.

"Yes. A little farther past the garnet plant. We should see the highway and the river takes a turn. This is a really small community."

"Good and bad. Let's go."

They continued on the tracks until it reached the road. Erin suggested a state park that included cabin rentals, and they walked the remaining mile and a half on tired legs, reaching the ranger station after closing.

"Better off," Dalton said. "No paper trail. Should be easy to see if any of the cabins are empty."

They walked the looped trail past occupied cabins, waving at other campers.

"I could set up my tent," said Erin.

"I need a shower," he said.

She agreed that he did. So did she, for that matter.

"Bathhouse?" he suggested.

"Let's finish the loop."

As it happened, the ranger was making rounds to invite guests to a talk on the reintroduction of wolves to the Adirondacks that started at nine. Erin asked the tanned ranger in his truck if any of the cabins were still unoccupied.

"You two hiking?"

"Yeah. Going into the Hudson Gorge Wilderness and up Vanderwhacker Mountain."

"We should be able to set you up."

"Cash okay?" asked Erin.

"That'll work."

They accepted a ride back down to the station. When the ranger asked for ID, Erin held her smile but her gaze flashed to Dalton.

"I have your wallet still, I think," he said, and offered the Vermont license of the woman who had killed the pair of campers, stolen their dog and then tried to kill them.

Erin remembered the hair the woman had commandeered and shuddered. The ranger listed them in his book but never ventured near a computer. They were Mrs. Kelly Ryder and her husband, Bob.

The ranger handed over a key on a lanyard and

Erin gave him seventy bucks. Transaction complete, Erin headed back out. Jet rose and stretched at their appearance. The ranger called from behind the counter.

"You'll need to put your dog on a leash."

Dalton waved his understanding as they left.

Cabin number eleven was a log structure with two bedrooms. Once inside, Erin removed her pack and groaned as she lowered her burden to the floor. Dalton flicked on the overhead light and glanced around at the living area, which included a full kitchen with a four-burner stove, refrigerator and small dinette. The living room had a saggy sleeper couch and a wooden rocker. A pair of crossed canoe paddles decorated the wall above the hearth made of river rock.

DALTON HEADED DOWN the hall past the living area and found a bathroom with toilet, sink and small shower. The first bedroom was equipped with bunks and the second with a full-size bed, dresser and side tables holding lamps with decoy bases that resembled wood ducks. He really hoped he wouldn't be sleeping alone in one of the bunks.

When he returned, Erin was staring at the stove with folded arms and a contemplative expression.

"Kinda makes me wish I had some food," she said as she looked at the stove.

"We have to eat," Dalton said. A glance out the window showed that the night was creeping in.

"How are you going to pull that off?" She sank to

the hard, wooden chair at the dinette and stared wearily at the knotty pine cupboards. Jet sat at her side and the dog rested her head in her new mistress's lap.

Erin stroked her dark head and said, "'Old Mother Hubbard went to the cupboard…'"

Dalton glanced out at the night. "I'll be right back."

He wasn't, but it didn't take him long. The ranger giving the talk was one of two, as he discovered upon knocking at the door to the rangers' quarters.

"I hate to bother you but those folks in cabin sixteen are shooting off bottle rockets. Guess the Fourth is coming early?"

The ranger cursed under her breath and headed out. Dalton waved her away and started off the porch, then retraced his steps after she drove off.

The door was unlocked and there were steaks in the freezer. He collected a paper bag full of groceries, left two twenty-dollar bills on the top of the drip coffee maker and headed out, returning to find Erin asleep on the sofa with her hiking boots unlaced but still on.

He didn't wake her. He let the smell of the steaks do that.

A few minutes later she opened one eye and then another. Her feet hit the floor and she rose stiffly to set the table.

"What have you got?"

He rattled off the menu. Fries and steaks, navel oranges and a box of chocolate-chip cookies. She started on those, offering Jet a one-to-three ratio on distribution, as Dalton tended the steaks.

"Where did you…never mind," she said. "I don't want to know."

He turned back to the steaks.

"Are these marshmallows?" She hefted the bag. "I love these!"

She had one toasting on a fork over the unoccupied burner of the gas stove as he used the salt and pepper before turning the meat. The only item of food in the cupboard other than salt and pepper was a ziplock baggie full of little packages of ketchup and mustard.

Dalton fed Jet from a box of breakfast cereal mixed with pan drippings and the gristle from the steaks. Then he put the dog outside without a leash.

They ate at the kitchen dinette.

Erin smiled across the table at him, and he realized he could not remember the last time he had cooked for her or even the last time they had shared supper together. His job kept him gone for long hours and took him away unexpectedly and often—far too often, he realized.

"This is nice," she said.

"I've missed this," he admitted.

Her smile turned sad. "Me, too."

"Erin, I never meant for my work to take over. I don't even know when that happened." He was never home before nine anymore. By the time he got on the train and made it back to the suburbs, Erin was often asleep on the couch. Her days began early at the sports club where she taught rock climbing with frequent weekend jaunts up to New Paltz, NY, to head rock climbing outings.

"Your partner will be here tomorrow?" she asked, finishing her last fry.

"He should be here already with the cavalry."

"Great. How far do we have to go to get to him?"

"North Creek."

"A couple of miles."

He nodded and then reached across the table to take her hand, but at the last second, he panicked and instead retrieved her plate. He stood to clear the table and she followed.

"Boy, am I stiff," she muttered, rolling her shoulders. The action forced her very lovely bosom out and he took that moment to stare. She caught him of course and laughed. "I'm surprised you have enough energy for that."

"Looking doesn't cost energy."

He recalled the last time he'd loved her, the evening before the shooting. He had hoped that she'd attend the ceremony, but he'd been too preoccupied with loving her before bed to remind her and she'd been up and out before he rose. He never did find out if she had planned to be at the presentation. He and his partner were both being honored at the annual medal day ceremony, so he had been in full dress uniform. That uniform now had a small hole in the front above his right hip. That was nothing compared to the holes in his body.

Erin called his uniform a target. That day, she'd been right. Targeted for no reason other than the uniforms they wore, and the shooter in custody after clearing his psych exam. Not crazy, just murderous over old grudges stretching back through his child-hood.

"Why don't you go shower?" he said. "I'll clean up."

She regarded him with mock surprise. "That's the sexiest thing you've said to me all day."

"The shower?" He couldn't help feeling hopeful.

"The cleanup." She dropped a quick kiss on his mouth and then spun away before he could reel her in. But she'd left him with something else.

Hope.

Hope for the night. Hope for their marriage.

He found himself humming as he went about clearing the table. The scratch at the door told him the canine had returned. He held the door open, but Jet danced off the porch and then paused on the spongy loam of pine needles, beyond the steps. She turned back, waiting.

The young female made a complete circle of the cabin, encouraging Dalton to do the same. He stepped out of the doorway, his instincts making him uncomfortable being backlit in the gap. He headed after Jet and discovered that the rear of the cabin stood on stout logs and, behind them, the hillside sloped steeply toward the ranger station. Usually he would have done a quick recon at a new place, but his fatigue and hunger had taken precedence.

The stars seemed bigger here and he took a moment to gaze up and enjoy their brilliance. It had been a long stretch between now and the last time he'd noticed them, but they'd been there waiting. On the side of the cabin, making his return route, he paused at the light streaming from the cozy structure and at the sound of the shower running. Water was gliding over his wife's beautiful naked body. And he was out here with the dog.

"Idiot," he muttered, and continued back to the porch.

He still didn't understand how getting ambushed while in uniform, and nearly dying, had split them up. He'd explained it was just one of those things, and that just made her madder.

He hadn't really thought of her having to attend Chris's funeral alone. Of having to speak to the widow, see his partner's children's faces as they lowered their father's coffin into the ground.

It scared her. He got that.

"Come on, Jet," he said, opening the door.

The dog streaked past him, so fast she was a moving shadow. Back inside, Jet was already on the couch.

"Better you than me, girl," he said, and left her there, hoping he could hold the towel for Erin.

She met him at the door, her hair a wet tangle and

her skin flushed pink. Steam billowed out behind her and she wore a clean white tank top and pink underwear. Both skimpy garments clung to her damp skin in a way that made his mouth go dry.

"It's all yours," she said, and slipped past him.

He caught her arm and she turned; her smile flickered and dropped away.

"Did you pick a room?" he asked.

"Yes?"

"Where do you want me?"

She lifted her chin, holding the power he'd given her.

"In my bed," she said.

He exhaled in relief. But she lifted a finger.

"We are still not okay, Dalton. You know that."

All he knew was that Erin would have him in her bed, and that seemed enough for now.

She regarded him with a serious expression that he could not read. He nodded and she left him the bathroom. He stripped and was in the narrow plastic compartment a moment later, leaving his clothing strewn across the floor. The water felt so good running over his sore muscles that he groaned. Then he washed away the sweat and grime. It seemed an eternity ago that he had showered in their small ranch-style home on a hill in Yonkers. Erin had left him a small liquid soap that was biodegradable for use on her hike. It barely foamed but did the job, leaving his skin with a tingle and the unfortunate scent of peppermint.

He scrubbed his scalp and the beard that had turned from a light stubble to the beginnings of something serious, and banged his elbows on the sides of the shower casing. The capsule had not been designed for a man who was over six feet and 245 pounds.

When he exited the shower, he found she'd left him only the tiny towel she used when hiking. It was the size of a gym towel, but he used it to dry off. Then he used her deodorant, toothbrush and toothpaste—one of the advantages of marriage, he thought, working out the tangles in his hair with a pink plastic comb the size of his index finger.

Dalton touched the three punctures in his abdomen left by the arthroscopy. Blood loss had been the biggest threat. The scars from the bullet were pink and puckered, but his stomach was flat and showed no bruising from the recent ordeal.

He glanced at his cargo pants, underwear and the shirt she had commandeered. All of it was filthy and he was not wearing any of it to bed. He did rinse out his T-shirt and boxers, hanging them on the empty towel rack to dry.

Erin knew he preferred to sleep in the nude. He retrieved only the firearms and the black zippered case containing the thumb drive and vial case. He used the minuscule towel to hide them in one broad hand as he glanced at himself in the mirror over the sink.

"Wish me luck," he said to himself.

He'd never needed it before with Erin. She'd always welcomed him, but that was before the shooting and all the fury it had kindled in her.

Dalton stepped into the room to find the light already switched off and Erin sitting up against the pillows. The room was cast in shadows. He navigated to her by the faint bluish light from the night sky. He sat on the opposite side of the bed from where she lay stretched out and seemingly naked beneath white sheets. He set the weapons and case on the bedside table. A glance told him that the weapon he'd given her sat on the table beside her.

"There was a packet of sheets and a woolen blanket on the bed," she said, explaining the bedding.

"Nice," he said, slipping in beside her.

She nestled against him and inhaled. "You smell like my soap," she said.

He wrapped an arm around her and drew her close, resting his cheek on the top of her head. Then he closed his eyes and thanked God that she was safe and here with him.

"We're lucky to be alive, you know?" she said.

"Same thought occurred to me. People were shooting at you and you weren't even wearing a uniform."

This comment was met with silence and he wondered what was wrong with him. Reminding her of why she was furious with him was not a great way to slip back into her good graces.

"Will you call your friend and tell him our location?"

"Yes. I'll head down to the ranger station and give a call."

"They have a phone?"

"An actual pay phone. Hard to believe."

"Can you even reverse the charges to a mobile phone?" she asked.

"I guess I'll find out."

"Wait here or come with you?" she asked.

"I'll only be a few minutes."

He kissed her forehead and was surprised when she looped her arms about his neck and kissed him the way she used to. Now he didn't want to leave, and he was certainly coming back as fast as humanly possible.

"I'll be quick."

She released him and he waited until he was outside before jogging to the station to make his call. Henry sounded relieved to hear his voice. He promised to be there in thirty minutes. Dalton wondered if that would be enough.

When he got back, he was greeted by Jet. Alarm bells sounded as he drew his weapon and searched, room by room for Erin. He found her in the bedroom, curled on the blanket. She opened her eyes at his appearance.

"Everything all right?"

"Yes. They'll be here within the hour."

He sank down beside her. His shoulders definitely drooped with the rest of him as the fatigue he had pushed aside finally caught up with him. And then he felt her hand on his thigh, sliding north with a sure path in mind. His shoulders lifted with the rest of him, and he rolled to his side.

"Erin, I've missed this."

"Doctor said you needed time to heal."

"I think we've established that I am healthy enough for sex."

"I'll be the judge of that," she said, and kissed him.

Her mouth demanded as her tongue sought access. Erin's kisses were so greedy and wild that they scared him a little. Her fervor pointed him toward fear.

Did she believe they would not get out of this?

The desperation of her fingers gripping his shoulders and her nails scoring his back told him that something had changed.

Early in their relationship, he and Erin had giggled and wrestled and enjoyed the fun and play of intimacy.

Now, after three years of marriage, they had fallen into a general pattern. He knew what she liked and gave it to her. He liked everything and was always happy when Erin wanted to try something new. But this wasn't new. It bordered on manic.

Her hands flew over his shoulders and then down the long muscles that flanked his spine. Nails raked his skin as her kisses changed from passion to something that lifted the hairs on his neck.

He drew back, extending his arms on either side of her head and stared down at his wife.

"Erin? You all right?"

"I don't know. I just want… I want…" Erin then did something she never did. She burst into tears. All the horror and the fear and the fight drained out of her, and she wept.

Dalton rolled to his side and gathered her up, stroking her back as she sobbed against his broad bare chest. She sprawled over him, limp and still except for her labored breathing and the cries that racked her body.

Jet arrived and poked Dalton's bare leg with her wet nose. That made him jump and caused Erin to lift her head.

"Dog scared me," he said, in explanation.

She turned her head and reached, patting the mattress. Jet did not hesitate. She leaped up beside her new mistress and licked her wet face.

Erin laughed, hugging the dog with one arm and him with the other. Then she released them both, nestling in beside him. Jet, seeming to feel the crisis averted, hopped from the bed and left the room.

"Erin, I'm going to get us out of this."

She said nothing.

"You don't think we're going to make it. Do you?"

"I've lost count of the times I thought we were both going to die. Whatever that thing is in that case you are hiding beside the bed, people are willing to kill for it."

"You still want me to leave it behind?"

He held his breath, waiting.

"No. My party died because of that thing, whatever it is. I've decided to see this through."

"For a minute I thought you were only willing to jump off trestle bridges after stray dogs."

"Jet isn't a stray. Her owners were murdered, just like my party." She lifted up on an elbow and stared down at him. Her hair fell across her face, shielding her expression from his view. She stroked his forehead with a thumb.

"I just want you to stay with me. You know?"

"Planning on it." He cradled her jaw in his hand, and she turned to press a kiss against his palm. "I've even signed up to take the civil service exam."

"You're going to be a supervisor?" Her voice held a squeak of elation that made him smile.

"Well, I can't run down crooks all my life."

She rested her head on his chest. "Oh, Dalton. That makes me so happy."

He didn't remind her that he still could be shot for just wearing his uniform, as was the case when he'd actually taken the bullet. Ironic that, when he had faced armed gunmen on the job, he'd never fired a round and that he'd escaped Afghanistan without catching lead, only to be shot at a red light.

And Erin wasn't immune from danger. She'd happened onto the worst of all situations, being the rabbit in a deadly game of chase.

He stroked his wife's drying hair as he calculated how far away Larson might be. The backup should be here anytime, and his friend was bringing the FBI, DHS and the New York State Police.

Odds were about to even up, he thought.

Dalton shut his eyes, determined to rest a few minutes before help arrived. But his eyes popped open when Erin slid up and over his body, straddling his hips as she indulged in a leisurely kiss that curled his toes.

Chapter Twelve

It had been too long, Erin thought as she deepened the kiss. Dalton's big body warmed her and she slid across him. His fingertips grazed her back and down over one hip, leaving a trail of tingling awareness.

His breathing rate increased, and she turned her head to allow them to snatch at the cool night air. Moonlight filtered through the glass window to splash across their naked bodies, revealing the tempting cording of his muscles as he caressed her.

Erin moved over him, showing him without words that she was ready for him, near desperate. He made a sound of surprise at her boldness as she took him, gliding over him to claim what was hers and remind him what he had missed.

The next sound he made was a strangled groan as his head fell back as he captured her hips in his broad, familiar hands. They rocked together in the night, savoring the perfect fit and rising desire. How had she ever thought that leaving this man would solve their problems?

She'd only increased them. Now she didn't know what to do. Except she knew she needed this, him, inside her and holding her and bringing her pleasure as he took his own.

He pulled her down against his chest, his hold becoming greedy as she reached her release, letting her cry tear from her throat and mingle with the sounds of the night.

Dalton arched, lifting her as she savored the receding echoes of pleasure and felt him reach his own. Together they fell, replete and panting, to the tangled bedsheets. Their slick bodies dried in the cool air. Their breathing slowed and Erin shivered. Dalton had reached for the blanket when something cold touched Erin's thigh.

She jumped. Dalton stilled, and a moment later the wet nose of their new addition poked him in the hip. Jet sat beside the bed, gazing up at the two of them as if asking if they needed anything.

"Jet," growled Dalton. "Git."

The dog stood, stretched and sauntered out the door.

Erin giggled. "How long was she there, do you think?"

Dalton threw an arm across his eyes. "I don't want to know."

Erin cuddled next to him and he dragged her close.

"I've missed you," he whispered. "Missed us."

"Me, too."

"I was so scared," he said.

She lifted up to see his face. Her husband was not scared of anything or anyone. It was one of the things she both loved and hated about him.

"Of what?"

"Losing you. Losing us."

She tried for a smile, but it felt sad right down to her belly, which was tightening in knots.

"I was scared, too. You were unconscious for so long and they said there might be brain damage. I thought you'd already left me."

He threaded his fingers in her hair. "I'm right here."

"This time."

They lay side by side on the sheets as the cool night air chilled their damp skin. Her husband was not only able to keep up with her on a cross-country hike and kayak rapids—he was able to keep up with her in bed.

His recovery was complete, and she smiled at the proof that all systems were up and running. Dalton had always made her see stars, but tonight he'd given her something more—hope for the future.

"So, we have a house and a dog," said Dalton. He left the rest unsaid. He'd been after her to get a dog, seeming to think that would fix his late-night absences and ease her loneliness. But it wasn't loneliness that kept her awake at night. It was fear of the day he couldn't come home.

And it had happened. And, somehow, they had both survived.

This time.

She was with him again and he was with her. They were a team, and together they would deliver this devil's package and hopefully help the authorities catch these dangerous maniacs of Siming's Army.

Only a few more minutes and they would be safe.

"We should get dressed," she muttered, her voice slow with the lethargy that gripped her.

"Yeah. We should."

They could head home with Jet, who she already considered an important part of her family. Dalton would pass the promotional exams and become a supervisor. Then she could stop looking at her phone as if it were the enemy and treating every knock on her door as if she were under attack.

Erin slipped from bed to use the bathroom and on her return, she cracked open the window in the bedroom. She liked to hear the wind blow through the big pines all about them and hear the peepers chorus. She lay back beside Dalton and closed her eyes, feeling happy and satisfied.

He'd finally heard her and was taking steps to do as she asked. She didn't want him to quit the force. She just wanted him around to collect his pension. And in the meantime, maybe they could talk about kids again. She knew Dalton wanted them. She just never felt safe enough to try.

Widows and orphans were seen to by the NYPD,

and that was only right. But she did not savor the prospect of joining their ranks. If Dalton wanted kids, he could darn well be there to raise them.

She had meant to get up and dressed, but instead she closed her eyes and drifted into a sleep like a feather falling to earth. She was in that deep sleep, the one that paralyzed you so that rousing felt like swimming up to the surface from deep water.

Someone was shaking her. She opened her eyes and looked around the dark room, struggling to get her bearings. From the hallway came the feral growl of a large animal.

"Dalton?" she whispered.

He pressed a pistol into her hand. "Get dressed."

"What's happening?" she said.

"Not sure. Jet hears something."

"Larson?"

"I don't think so."

She was about to ask who Jet was and where they were when the entire thing dropped into place. Her hairs lifted and the lethargy of sleep flew off. Her heart pummeled her ribs, and she sat up so fast her head spun.

The breeze from the window had turned cold and she was suddenly regretting opening it. The cabin was perched on a slope, so crawling in the window would be difficult—but not impossible.

"Have they found us?" she asked.

"Not sure. Might be a raccoon. Porcupine."

Or a man, she realized.

Dalton disappeared and returned carrying her pack and wearing his cargo pants and shirt. He sat on the bed for the few seconds it took to tug on his boots.

She set aside the gun to scramble into jeans, shirt, jacket and socks, and then realized her boots were in the living room.

"My boots are out there." She pointed.

"Come on," he said, offering his hand.

"Take the pack?"

"For now."

They reached the hallway and Erin called Jet's name just above a whisper. The dog came immediately and Erin grabbed her collar. Her hand at Jet's neck relayed that every hair on the dog's neck was standing straight up.

"Her hackles," she whispered.

"Yeah. Mine, too," he said.

Something large flew through the front window. Dalton lifted his pistol and aimed as the log rolled across the living room floor.

"They're trying to force us to go out the back," he said. "Safer than coming in here."

"They? Just how many are there?" Erin snatched up her boots. Quickly, she tugged them on.

He crept toward the door and the automatic gunfire exploded in the night.

"Down!" roared Dalton, and she fell to her stomach, sprawling as bullets tore through the frame and door.

FREE BOOKS GIVEAWAY

GET TWO FREE BOOKS & TWO FREE GIFTS WORTH OVER $20!

We pay for everything!

Complete the survey below and return it today to receive 2 FREE BOOKS and FREE GIFTS guaranteed!

FREE BOOKS GIVEAWAY
Reader Survey

1
Do you prefer stories with suspenseful storylines?

◯ YES ◯ NO

2
Do you share your favorite books with friends?

◯ YES ◯ NO

3
Do you often choose to read instead of watching TV?

◯ YES ◯ NO

YES! Please send me my Free Rewards, **2 Free Books** and **Free Mystery Gifts**. I understand that I am under no obligation to buy anything, as explained on the back of this card.

❏ I prefer the regular-print edition
182/382 HDL GNVY

❏ I prefer the larger-print edition
199/399 HDL GNVY

FIRST NAME   LAST NAME

ADDRESS

APT.#   CITY

STATE/PROV.   ZIP/POSTAL CODE

BUSINESS REPLY MAIL
FIRST-CLASS MAIL   PERMIT NO. 717   BUFFALO, NY

POSTAGE WILL BE PAID BY ADDRESSEE

READER SERVICE
PO BOX 1341
BUFFALO NY 14240-8571

NO POSTAGE
NECESSARY
IF MAILED
IN THE
UNITED STATES

Jet tugged against her, trying to break free.

"Two shooters, at least," said Dalton. "Get to the bedroom."

The gunfire came again as she scrambled down the hall, dragging her pack in one hand and Jet by the collar in the other. Then something else flew through the open window. She heard the object hit the wood floor and shatter, and the acrid tang of gasoline reached her.

"Molotov cocktail," he said.

She glanced back. Fire erupted in the living room. A log cabin, with wooden walls and wooden floors. How long until the entire place was ablaze?

"Forcing us back," he said, following her into the bedroom and closing the door against the wall of fire.

"What do we do?" she said.

Dalton moved to the window, keeping low, but the moment he lifted his head someone started shooting. He ducked back down.

"Are you hit?" she said, unable to keep the panic from her voice as she crawled to him, dragging Jet along.

Smoke now billowed under the closed door. Dalton dragged the wool blanket off the bed and stuffed it against the base of the door.

"They've got infrared," he said.

"How do you know that?"

"Because he just missed my head and I can't see a thing."

Smoke continued to creep around the door.

"We have to use the window."

Footsteps sounded in the hall. The second shooter was out there. Bullet holes riddled the bedroom door and Dalton rolled clear of the opening, crouching beside her near the bed.

"When he opens the door, let go of the dog."

The shooter kicked the door open and Erin released her hold on Jet's collar. The dog moved like a streak of black lightning. The shooter fired as Jet jumped, knocking the intruder back. Erin held her breath as both intruder and canine vanished in the smoke.

Dalton charged after the dog with his pistol raised. She lost them in the smoke but clearly heard two shots. A moment later, Dalton emerged from the billowing smoke with Jet at his heels and kicked the door shut. In his hands was a semiautomatic rifle.

The shooter outside opened fire as Jet reached Erin. She swept a hand over the dog's coat, searching for the sticky wetness that would tell her that Jet had been shot. But her hands came away dry.

Dalton reached her. "I'm going to knock out that window. Then I want you to let the dog go again."

"He'll kill her."

Dalton said nothing for a moment. "She's fast. She's black and the shooter won't be expecting it. Jet's our only chance."

Erin did not want to die in this cabin.

"All right."

Dalton threw her pack outside. Gunfire erupted and then ceased.

"Now!"

She released Jet, who jumped out the window and vanished. Dalton went next. She heard him land. Then came the sound of someone screaming and shots firing.

Afterward there was only the crackling sound of burning wood.

"Erin! Clear! Come out the window."

She choked on tears and on smoke as she groped for the opening, grabbed hold of the sill and dropped to the ground some seven feet below. The slope sent her into an unanticipated roll that ended with her flat on her back against the roots of a tree.

Jet reached her first. Her dog licked her face until she sat up and then the dog charged away, likely back to Dalton.

"Where are you?" she called.

Dalton called back. She stood then and fell over her backpack. She groaned as every muscle in her back seemed to seize, but she righted herself and headed toward her husband's voice, carrying the pack over one shoulder.

Jet raced to her and then away. Behind her, the light from the blazing cabin illuminated the hillside. Sparks flew up into the sky, and she prayed that the ground was still wet enough to keep this fire from spreading to the forest surrounding them.

"Did you get him?" she asked.

"Yes."

Dalton returned up the hill for her and took hold of the pack, then dashed down the slope away from the fire.

"Shouldn't we wait for fire and police?"

"I'm not certain there aren't more of them." He tugged her along.

The ground was dark, and she stumbled over roots and through shrubs.

"If there are more, they can just pick us off from the woods."

"But if we get to the police."

Dalton didn't slow. "I don't know them. I know my people. We need to get to them."

They reached the other side of the roundabout on the cabin road and he paused, waiting. She heard the engine sound a moment later. Jet sat beside her and she grabbed her collar.

"She saved our lives," she said, and stroked Jet's soft head with her free hand.

"Yesterday she nearly cost you yours, so we're even."

She recalled her jump from the bridge.

"She fell."

Dalton said nothing as he watched the ranger's truck sweep past.

"How are you planning to get out of here?"

Chapter Thirteen

Dalton doubled back and waited as other cabin dwellers gathered at a distance from the fire. He watched them, looking for some sign that one or more were armed. The first to arrive were the rangers, who quickly disconnected the propane tank outside the kitchen window and dragged it away.

They told everyone to keep back and asked if the two in the cabin had made it out. He waited with Erin outside the circle of light cast by the flames until the fire department and state police arrived. Only then did Dalton leave cover. He made straight for the police. Erin followed, despite his order for her to wait She left her pack and the automatic weapon behind.

Dalton scanned the crowd. Everyone seemed intent on watching the cabin blaze. He worried about the surrounding dark. A sniper could pick them off with ease.

"What happened?" asked a park ranger. "Stove blow?"

Dalton pulled Erin down so that the ranger's

pickup truck was between them and the woods above the cabin. Before them, flames shot out of the windows and smoke curled onto the roof of their cabin.

"I heard gunfire," said a woman in pink yoga pants and an oversize T-shirt.

"Automatic gunfire," added the tall, balding guy holding a half-finished cigarette.

The group clustered together, arms folded as they watched the firefighters set up. Erin held Jet and squatted beside a rear tire.

"Can you wait here just a minute?" Dalton asked.

She hesitated, chewing a thumbnail. "Where are you going?"

He pointed to the well-built trooper, his hat sloped forward revealing the bristle on the back of his head. He was tall and broad shouldered, wearing a crisp uniform with a black utility belt complete with all appropriate gear.

"That guy is the real deal. I'd bet my life on it," he said.

"Good, because you're about to."

"I'll be right back," he said.

"You said there might be more of them out here."

"We need help, Erin."

She stood and shouted, "Mr. State Trooper. I need help."

The trooper turned and looked their way. Erin waved.

"Over here."

The officer strode toward them. Dalton had to smile. Erin had gotten help without leaving cover.

"Yes, ma'am?" said the trooper. He was young, Dalton realized, without a line on his baby face. Still, he stood with one hand casually near his weapon and eyes alert.

Dalton identified himself to the trooper as an NYC detective and showed the officer his gold shield. Then he quickly described the situation.

"Two dead. One in the cabin and one behind the cabin."

The trooper lifted his radio. "Wait here."

"If you use that radio, anyone listening will know our position. Call it in with your phone."

The trooper hesitated, then nodded. "That your dog?" His gaze went to Jet, who sat calm and alert beside Erin.

Erin slipped an arm about Jet, suddenly protective.

"Is now," said Dalton. "Why?"

"Do you know anything about a couple murdered in the Hudson Gorge Wilderness? They were camping with a black dog."

"Plenty," said Dalton.

Erin interrupted. "Did you find a teenage boy, Brian Peters. He was in my party?"

"Not that I'm aware of. But we do have a missing party of adult kayakers."

"That's my party," said Erin, pressing her palm flat to her chest. "I was the expedition leader."

"Erin Stevens?" asked the trooper.

"Yes. That's me."

"Where is the rest of your party?" asked the trooper.

Erin burst into tears.

Dalton took over. "I was with them when their camp was attacked. We escaped with the boy, Peters. He suffered a gunshot wound to his upper arm, couldn't hold a paddle. My wife towed him to the opposite bank from her camp and gave him instructions on how to walk out, then she and I proceeded downriver. The rest of her party aren't missing. They're dead."

"No evidence of that."

"There is. And there is a downed chopper in the river below the cliff."

"I'm going to need to bring you both in."

"Sounds good to me. Can you get some backup? I'm not sure that there aren't more out here."

"Who's after you?"

"Long story. You need to send help after Peters. Also, I need you to call New York City detective Henry Larson. He's here in North Creek. That was our destination."

"You can call from the station." He aimed a finger at them. "Wait here."

Dalton watched him stride away. It seemed to take hours, but he suspected it was less than forty-five minutes before they were transported to Trooper Barracks G in Queensbury. Another thirty minutes and four FBI agents arrived with two beefy guys from DHS.

It was five in the morning and the knot in Dalton's shoulders finally began to ease. They had made it. They were safe, though he still had the package.

Erin and he were separated, something that rankled and made him anxious. He felt the need to keep looking out for her, regardless of how many times she'd proved her own capabilities. He went over the events with the FBI agents Nolen Bersen and Peter Heller. Bersen took lead. He was tall, fit and had hair that was cut so brutally short it seemed only a shadow on his head. Heller stood back, arms folded, his freckled forehead furrowed beneath a shock of hair so red that it appeared to be illuminated from within.

By six thirty in the morning Dalton needed the bathroom and some food. He was informed that Henry Larson had been notified that they were now safe and had arrived, but Dalton could not see him. In the bathroom he discovered he was not to have a moment's privacy when a Homeland Security agent, Lawrence Foster, flashed his ID. He wanted a word. Dalton told him to get in line.

"Do you still have the package?" asked Foster.

This was the first person who seemed to know anything about the intelligence he and Erin had rescued. Dalton used the urinal and ignored him until he was finished. Then he faced the guy, who was heavyset with close-cropped hair, brown skin and dressed like an attorney in a well-fitting suit.

Dalton narrowed his eyes on the man. He knew all about interagency competition. His office hated it when the FBI came and took over an operation or, worse, took their collar. So he understood Foster's attempt to get something but still resented his choice of time and place.

"This is my first time being interviewed in a toilet," said Dalton. "You want to join us in interrogation room three, come on along."

Foster smiled and stepped away from the door he had been blocking. "I'll see you there."

Dalton headed back to the interrogation room. It was nearly eight when the room was cleared of everyone but two men in plain clothes. The elder one stepped forward. Dalton guessed him to be just shy of forty, with close cropped salt-and-pepper hair, going gray early. He wore a slouch hat, fisherman's-style shirt, worn jeans and muddy sneakers. At first glance, he looked as if he'd been hauled off an angling excursion. Second glance made Dalton's skin crawl. He'd worked with CIA, and this guy had that look.

His gaze flicked to the younger man. This one would fit in almost anywhere. He was slim, with a thick beard, glasses and hair that brushed his collar. His clothing was banal, jean shorts and a white tee worn under a forest green plaid cotton shirt. He could be pumping gas or passing you at the horse race track. The point was you wouldn't notice him. The guy's gaze finally flicked to Dalton, and those intent gray eyes gave a whole other picture. A chill danced along the ridge of his spine.

"What agency?" asked Dalton.

"Federal," replied the older guy. His cap said he'd fought in Operation Iraqi Freedom, but somehow Dalton thought he was still active. "You got something that you want to give to us?"

"I don't know what you mean."

The men exchanged a look.

"Let's start again. We were expecting the delivery of some sensitive material. Our courier delivered that information successfully to one of our operatives. The helicopter he was flying crashed into your wife's party, killing Carol Walton."

"You all clean up that scene?"

He nodded.

"Terrible tragedy. Surprised you made it out. Looked professional. Helicopter, according to reports."

"You CIA?"

The second man took that one. "We are here to see just how much you know. Clearly you know something because you ran, survived, and we have not recovered our package. Judging from the trail of bodies, neither have your pursuers. Though, close one tonight."

"You recovered the two that came after us?"

"Bagged and tagged," said the Iraqi vet. "How

did you end up with our intelligence and do you still have it?"

Dalton ground his teeth together for a few seconds, opened his mouth. Closed it again and then wiped it.

His initial interviewer passed him something. He drew back, leaving a folded sheet of paper on the desk. Dalton looked from the page to the man across from him at the table. Then he lifted the paper and read the contents of the letter.

It was from his direct supervisor returning him to active duty and notifying him that he was on loan to a Jerome Shaffer. Dalton recognized the signature. His gaze flicked up to the Iraqi vet, who had removed his wallet from his back pocket and laid a laminated ID card before him.

This was Jerome Shaffer and he worked, according to the card, with the Central Intelligence Agency.

The two stared at each other from across the table.

"I need to hear it from my boss."

The call was made and a sleepy, familiar voice verified that Dalton was now on loan to the CIA until further notice. He handed back the phone.

"Okay," he said.

Agent Shaffer nodded. "So where is it?"

Dalton opened the side pocket of his cargo pants and laid the black leather case on the table.

Both men stiffened. Shaffer rose and they backed toward the door.

"Don't move," said Shaffer. A moment later the

pair were in the hallway and the door between him and the agents closed firmly shut. The click told him he was locked in the interrogation room. He looked to the mirrored glass, knowing there were others out there, but as he could not see them, he still didn't know what was going on.

Fifteen minutes later the door swung open and in stepped a woman in a full hazmat suit.

Chapter Fourteen

They had separated Erin from Dalton shortly after their arrival at the troopers' headquarters. Dalton told her it would be all right, but as the minutes ticked by she became restless and had just given up pacing in the small interrogation room in favor of drinking from the water bottle they had furnished.

She looked up as the door clicked open, hoping to see Dalton. Instead, a trooper stepped in, preceding two men who were not in uniform.

Erin lowered the bottle to the table.

The trooper made introductions and Erin shook hands with each in turn. Agent Kane Tillman was first. He wore business casual, loafers and tan pants with a gray sports coat and a classic tie on a pale blue shirt. His face was cleanly shaven and his short hair had a distinctly military air.

Agent Tillman said he was a government investigator of some sort. She missed his title as the other man offered his hand. His associate was more unkempt with hair neither stylish nor unfashionable.

His clothing was as drab as his features. She glanced away from him after the introduction and realized she'd only heard part of his name. Gabriel. Was that his first or last name?

She assumed that they were FBI agents, though Gabriel was not dressed like the other FBI agent, Jerome Shaffer, whom she had met on arrival. Her gaze slid to Gabriel. Was his hair dark blond or light brown? She wasn't sure, but Agent Tillman was speaking, so she turned her attention back to him.

They told her that they'd spoken to Dalton and that she'd be allowed to see him soon. The best news was that Brian Peters had been found alive.

"He was picked up by a ranger and driven to their station. We took charge of him from there."

"His wounds?"

"Superficial. He'll make a full recovery."

She sank back in her seat as relief washed through her, closing her eyes for a moment before the questions began again.

Her interviewer wanted to hear about the helicopter crash.

She relayed to Agent Tillman all she recalled of the attempted rescue of the pilot. They told her the pilot was a friend. Agent Tillman said that he'd known the man, and so Erin had been thorough. The other man, she could not recall his name now, only the letter *G*. The other one listened but rarely spoke.

"And he said to tell the authorities what exactly?"

"He said to tell you this was taken from Siming's Army."

"Right. And he gave you something?"

"Yes, a cooler."

"Which your husband carried."

"At first. Then he just carried the contents. We left the cooler to throw our pursuers off us."

"You believe they were after what you carried?"

She reported what they had overheard before running for their lives.

"Right," said Tillman. "We were looking for you, as well. Seems you outfoxed both pursuing parties. Even our dogs couldn't find you."

She shrugged. "Rain helped. We only left the river day before yesterday. I'm glad you didn't stop us. I'm afraid Dalton might have thought you were one of our attackers."

Tillman just smiled. "Well, this is better."

"Will we be able to go home?"

Tillman's smile grew tight. "I'm afraid not quite yet. You see, all the opponents you two faced are dead. But we believe there are several more in the region. We are very anxious to capture someone from this organization."

"I see." She didn't, and her face twisted in confusion. Why was he telling her this?

"Your husband has agreed to go back to the Hudson. He will be helping us catch the people who tracked you."

Her eyes narrowed. "Helping how?"

"He's a detective. He's worked undercover. We think it's our best option."

Erin straightened in her chair as her gaze flicked from one to the other.

"He said that?"

Tillman didn't answer directly. "He'll explain the details to you."

Something stank. Either he was lying or Dalton was ignoring every promise he'd made to her.

"What about his wife? He wasn't out there alone. Don't you think they'll notice that I'm no longer there?"

The other guy spoke and she jumped. She'd half forgotten he was even in the room and now he was right next to her, leaning against the wall beside the door.

"That's no problem."

What color were his eyes? she wondered, squinting. Green, gray, blue? It was hard to tell and he was only two feet from her.

He was smiling at her. It was an unpleasant smile that raised the hairs on her forearms.

"We have a substitute. Someone to play your part."

"The hell you say." She stood and faced them. "We just spent two days running for our lives and you want him to go back there without me? Phooey on that!"

"It's our best option."

"I want to speak to him now," she said, arms folding.

"Not possible," said Tillman.

"Now," she said, leaning across the table, looking for a fight.

Tillman backed toward the door. The other guy was already gone. She rushed the closing door.

"I want to see him!"

Tillman shut the door before she reached it, and the lock clicked behind him. Tugging on the handle only made her remember how sore her muscles were.

They allowed her to leave the vile little room to use the bathroom, escorted by a female trooper with umber skin and unusual height.

"I want to see my husband."

"I'll relay the message," she said.

"Where is my dog?"

"They are processing her for evidence."

"If you hurt one hair…"

The threat was cut short as the athletic woman lifted a thin eyebrow.

"She has bloodstains on her collar. They are taking samples."

Back in the interrogation room she found only the empty chairs and table. She walked to the one-way mirror and slapped it.

"I want my husband or my phone call now!" Who would she call? The camp director? She snorted and began her pacing again.

Tillman opened the door and motioned to someone in the hallway. In stepped a slim, athletic woman of a similar height to her.

Erin glared at the new arrival.

"Mrs. Stevens, this is DHS agent Rylee Hockings out of Glens Falls."

"My substitute," said Erin, standing to face her replacement. "She has blue eyes and she's blond."

"Contacts. Hair dye," said Tillman.

From the sidelong look Agent Hockings cast him, Erin guessed no one had told her about the dye job.

"It's a pleasure to meet you, Erin." Hockings extended her hand. Unlike Erin's hand, Hockings's was dirt-free, her nails trimmed into uniformed ovals and coated with a pale pink polish. She was clean and smelled wonderful.

"Look at her." She swept her hand at Hockings and then at herself. "Now look at me."

Erin wore damp, rumpled clothing and hair tugged into a messy ponytail. She knew she had circles under her eyes. She smelled of smoke and gasoline, and there were numerous scratches on her shins and forearms.

"I look like I spent the night in a bramble bush. But she looks like she just left a resort hotel."

Tillman's mouth went tight, but he said nothing.

Erin faced her replacement. "Have you been camping, Ms. Hockings? Do you know how to kayak in white water or set up a climbing rope?"

"I doubt that will be necessary."

"But it *was* necessary. Or I wouldn't be here."

Hockings glanced to Tillman, who offered no backup. So Hockings straightened her shoulders.

"I can fill this role, Erin."

"You are asking me to trust you to keep my husband alive. I don't think so."

"I'm an excellent shot."

"He's got that one covered all on his own."

Tillman stepped in. Erin had crept forward and was now right up in the agent's face. Funny, she didn't remember even moving closer.

"This isn't your call, Erin. She'll be in the field in less than one hour with or without your help. All you get to decide is if you help Hockings prepare or not?"

"Not," said Erin as she returned to her seat, folded her arms and scowled.

The two retreated out the door, leaving her alone again.

THE DOOR TO the interrogation room opened, and Dalton turned to see both the small blond DHS agent and the CIA operative. Both of them were flushed. He stood for introductions. The woman, Rylee Hockings, chewed her bottom lip, and Kane Tillman had both hands clamped to his hips.

Dalton narrowed his eyes on them, speculating. Who did he know that could rattle both DHS and CIA?

He smiled. "You spoke to my wife."

Tillman nodded, removing his hands from his hips to lock his fingers behind his neck and stretch. He dropped his arms back to his sides and faced Dalton.

"Can you point out to us your route and specifically your position yesterday when you encountered the female shooter?"

Dalton's smile broadened. "Nope."

"The general location?" asked Rylee, hope flickering weakly in her gaze.

"Out of sight of the Hudson River on a hill." Dalton chuckled at their dismay. "I told you. You need her."

Tillman said nothing.

"She agree to help?" Dalton asked.

He shook his head. "She wants to see you."

"I told you it wouldn't work."

"You need to convince her to cooperate with us," said Hockings.

"You know that she asked for a separation. Right?" he asked Tillman.

"Yes."

"Do you know why?"

Tillman shook his head.

"Because I go undercover and stay away for days. She wants me to ride a desk and collect my pension. What she doesn't want is for me to play secret agent with a younger model who—no offense, Miss Hockings—looks like she does most of her traveling first-class."

"Business class," corrected Hockings.

"But not in the woods carrying a fifty-pound pack on your back."

"I can fill this role." She was speaking to Tillman now.

Dalton had told them that lying to his wife about his cooperation was a bad idea and that he wouldn't go without her consent, but they'd thought to trick it out of her.

He smiled. Erin was many things—stubborn, driven, protective—but not stupid.

"My wife rescued that helicopter pilot. Not me. She swam through white water, rigged him so we could haul him out and then got out herself, even though the wreck rolled on her tether rope. She got us downriver, through rapids. It was her idea to leave the kayaks on the opposite side of the river, to throw them off our trail, in the pouring rain."

"All very admirable."

"I told you that she won't want me to go back."

"You don't need her permission."

"No. But I'm not going without it."

"I don't understand. You're a professional."

"I'm a man about to lose his wife. I came up here to fix my marriage. Now you want me to go right back to telling her to wait at home and that everything will be fine when the last time I told her that I caught a bullet."

Tillman's hands slid back to his hips.

"We all know that these people are crazy, armed and dangerous," said Dalton. "She knows, too, firsthand."

"You willing to risk her life?"

"Heck no. But we have both been convinced of the importance of this. I think she should have a choice. She's right. I've asked her to sit on the sidelines too

long. I wouldn't like it. Neither does she. I understand now why she didn't like it. Why she's been so
angry. My thick head has been an asset in the past.
But I don't want it to end my marriage."

"So what are you suggesting?" asked Tillman.

"Get her to help or let us go home."

Tillman looked at Hockings. "Sorry for dragging
you up here. Seems we don't need you after all."

"This is bull," said Rylee. "I can do this job."

"We'll never know." He turned to Dalton. "That
is assuming you can convince your wife to help us."

"She'll do what she thinks is best."

"For you or for her country?"

"Let's go find out. Shall we?"

Chapter Fifteen

The door had barely closed behind DHS agent Lawrence Foster when it opened again, this time to admit Hockings, Shaffer, Tillman and her husband. Erin kept her face expressionless as she met Dalton's gaze but was relieved to see him. Something about DHS agent Foster had put her on edge. His questions were off, somehow, different from the others who had questioned her. Dalton winked at her and she could not keep the half smile from lifting her mouth.

"You going back there without me?" she asked.

Dalton turned to the three agents. "Give us a minute."

The two exchanged impatient looks.

"We don't have a lot of time," said Tillman.

"Understood," said Dalton. He wasn't looking at Tillman, and only Erin watched the others retreat and close the door behind them.

"I hear you've been less than cooperative with our

federal friends," Dalton said, and drew up a chair beside her.

"I was cooperative with the DHS agent." She'd answered all his questions about the pilot's death, their escape and details about the woman who attacked them. He asked what was in the package that Dalton carried, and she told him it was vials and a thumb drive. The agent then asked about Dalton's colleague, Henry Larson, or "the NYPD SWAT officer," as Foster had called him. Maybe that was the thing that bothered her. Why didn't he know Larson's name?

"You weren't cooperative with the CIA," said Dalton.

"Because Agent Foster wasn't trying to replace me."

Dalton made a growling sound in his throat by way of reply that showed both skepticism and some aggravation. Then he took her hand and entwined her fingers with his.

"What should we do, Erin?"

"Don't ask me to let you go back there," she said.

"I won't," he said.

That got her attention. She waited, but he said nothing else. Just stroked his thumb over the sensitive skin at the back of her hand at the web between her index finger and thumb.

"They want to send you out with that woman."

"Yeah. They do."

"So you're going back without me," she said.

"That what they told you?" he asked.

She nodded.

"And what have I told you about interrogation techniques?"

Her brow knit and then arched. "You don't have to tell a suspect the truth." She let out a breath and drew another. "They lied? To me?"

She smiled, but instead of returning her smile he was frowning.

"And you believed them."

"You've run off on dangerous business for years. Why wouldn't I believe them?"

"Because I told you that I wouldn't do that again."

Now she shifted, suddenly uncomfortable with the man she had once felt was an extension of herself. They'd moved apart now, like heavenly bodies changing their orbits. She wanted to align with him once more. Why was this so hard?

"What did you tell them?" she asked.

"I told them it's a bad idea to send our Ms. Hockings as your replacement."

She cocked her head. "You did? Why?"

"Because she can't fill your hiking boots. Because our pursuers are not stupid, and because I promised you that I wouldn't go out there."

"Without me."

Now he was off balance. She knew from the way he tilted his head as he narrowed his eyes. "What are you saying, Erin?"

"You think this is worth risking your life for?"

"I do."

"You ready to risk *my* life, too?" she asked.

"No," he said.

"Yet you think the information they could get from a living member of Siming's Army would be invaluable," she said.

"That information could save the lives of many innocent people. Might stop whatever is underway. But that is only if we manage not to get killed and they manage to capture someone alive."

"You believe they can keep us safe?"

"I believe they will try. But I don't think they can keep us safe *and* allow the bad guys to get close. So..." He lifted his hands, palms up as if weighing his options.

"They'll put us in danger."

"I'd say so."

"Thank you," she said.

"For being honest?"

"For not going without me."

"I'm done with that," he said.

"And I'm sorry for believing them."

He nodded, but the hurt still shone in his troubled gaze.

"Are we still okay?" he asked.

She forced out a breath between closed lips. "Let's talk about this after. Assuming there is an after."

"Erin, I came up here to save our marriage."

She nodded. "I know it. But trouble just has a way of finding you."

"Seems this time it found you."

Erin looked at the ceiling, taking a moment to rein herself in. They did not have time to hash out their differences. He might have told her that he was done taking chances and willing to change. But all actions pointed to the contrary.

"Where are they taking us?"

"Heck if I know. You know I can't read a map as well as you."

She rose then, went to the door and knocked. When Tillman's face appeared in the window, she motioned him inside.

"We've agreed to go back." She glanced at Dalton. "Together."

Rylee Hockings pressed her lips flat, exhaled like a horse through her nostrils and then stormed away down the hall, back to wherever she had come from, Erin hoped. Erin would not be sad to see the backs of either of the DHS agents—Hockings or Foster. One made her angry and the other gave her the creeps.

Tillman pressed a phone to his ear. "Yeah. They're in."

THE STEVENSES WERE left just outside the Hudson Gorge Wilderness on North Woods Club Road between the Boreas River and the small community of Minerva. This was the same side of the river where they had left the body of their female attacker and a reasonable distance for them to have traveled after that encounter. The dog, Jet, had remained back with their handlers. So at least one of them was safe.

Erin hefted her pack, knowing it was lighter but still thinking it felt heavier than before. Dalton carried the case of vials and thumb drive in his side pocket just as he had before. Only now the new thumb drive was inoperable due to irreparable damage and the vials were full of water.

"So we just use the road, after spending all that time keeping in cover?" asked Erin.

"That's the best way to be spotted."

"It doesn't make sense. We wouldn't do that, not after being attacked."

"At some point you have to leave cover and get help," he said.

"They said they'd keep us in sight," said Erin. "But there is no one here."

"How do you know?" he asked.

"Insects still singing. Jays and red squirrels aren't giving any alarm."

"It's a drone and it's up high enough that we can't hear it. But it surely can see us."

They also wore trackers. She had several. The coolest by far were in the earring posts she now wore.

"They might just shoot us and then search our bodies," she said.

Dalton groaned. "You are such a drop of sunshine today."

"Well, we don't have vests or armor, whatever you call it."

"Car," he said.

"What?"

He pointed to the rooster tail of dust growing by the second. It turned out to be a silver pickup truck. The driver came from the opposite direction. He slowed at sighting them but merely lifted two fingers off the steering wheel in a lazy wave as he passed them.

"Well, that was anticlimactic," Erin said.

"Could be a spotter."

She hadn't thought of that.

"Did Tillman tell you anything that I didn't hear?" she asked.

"Don't think so."

"So, this guy, this Japanese agent."

"Yes. A Japanese operative working out of Hong Kong," he said.

"Right," she said. "Hong Kong, which is where he obtained this information and put it on our flash drive."

"And he had the samples."

"Which he put on a commercial jet with hundreds of people and flew all the way to Canada."

"Toronto."

"And then, instead of meeting our government's agent, he changes the meeting to Ticonderoga."

"Fort Ticonderoga," said Dalton.

"See, that's why I'm going over this. You're the detail guy."

Dalton took it from there. "But they are attacked

during the drop. Our guy gets away. Their agent takes off and leaves the country. The foreign agents chase our guy all over the place, but he made the pickup anyway and they send a chopper."

"And he makes the drop. But the helicopter— our helicopter—takes gunfire and goes down on my camping site."

"And queue the chase music. Both parties have been after us ever since."

"This Siming's Army seems more like a foreign agency."

"Backed by one."

"Which one?" she asked.

"They didn't say."

"To me, either." Erin rubbed the back of her neck. "Did they say how many people they have?"

"Sleeper cells, so it's hard to know. But you just imagine that they have people downstate. NYC is a target and it's my city. Damned if I'll let that happen if I can prevent it."

"If we can prevent it."

He wrapped an arm around her and gave a squeeze. "We."

"Did you tell them about the pilot? I heard him mention his girl."

"Yes, Sally. I told them. They'll speak to her. Relay his last words."

"Good. But it's so sad."

She heard the engine, the same truck returning toward them. The driver slowed and lowered his window. Erin stared at the face of a man in his middle years. His hat advertised the sports club that lay at the terminus of this road, but she knew the distance and he had not had time to have reached it and returned. The niggling apprehension woke in her chest, squeezing tight as her skin crawled. She shifted from side to side, unable to keep still.

"So we just let them take us?" she asked.

"That's right."

"What if they just shoot us?"

"I won't let that happen."

"Still time to run," she said, edging off the shoulder, eyeing the distance to the trees.

The truck stopped and the dust caught up, drifting down on them in a haze.

"Hey there," called the driver, keeping his hands on the wheel. Between his arms was a small, overweight dog that seemed to be both smiling and preparing to steer the truck. Her gaze flicked up to the man to note that he was clean shaven, with salt-and-pepper hair that touched his shoulders, making a veil from under his cap. His glasses were thick and black rimmed.

"You two need a lift?"

Accent was right, Erin thought.

"Appreciate it," said Dalton. His voice was calm and even.

Erin doubted she was even capable of speech. She was good at the game of hide-and-seek, but less comfortable with the bravado required for confrontation.

She thought of Rylee Hockings and straightened her spine. Her feet stilled and her jaw tightened.

Dalton moved to the truck, opening the passenger-side door. He motioned to Erin.

She spoke to the driver, her voice a squeaky, un-recognizable thing. "Okay if I put the pack in the back?"

"Sure thing."

Dalton took the pack and placed it in the truck bed. When he turned around, he had his pistol in his hand. He slid that hand back into his pocket and motioned for her to get in.

Dalton slipped in beside her and pulled the door shut.

"This here is Lulu. She's my copilot," said the driver.

The small pug moved to sniff Erin and then used her as a boardwalk to sniff Dalton's extended hand. She wondered if the canine smelled gun oil.

"Where you two heading?" The driver flicked on his wipers to push away the settling dust from his windshield and then set them in motion.

"Minerva."

"Oh, that's right on my way."

Erin let Dalton do the small talk. He'd always been better at it. She focused on the driver's hands as she wondered what he had in the pockets of his denim jacket.

"Surprised to see you two out here."

"Why's that?" asked Dalton.

"Ain't ya heard about the trouble?"

"No."

"Where you been then, you ain't seen the helicopters and K-9 units. Yesterday this place looked like a TV movie set with all the cop cars. They all showed up like buzzards circling a dead woodchuck."

"Why? What happened?" Dalton asked.

"I don't know how to tell you this, but there's some maniac out here killing campers in their tents. Husband and wife. Right down that way on the trail to the trestle bridge."

Erin tried to look shocked but felt her face burning. This was why she had landed nothing more than chorus in the high school plays. Her acting left so much to be desired.

"That's terrible," she managed.

"That ain't all. There's a whole party of kayakers two days overdue. DEC's been out searching, but so far they're just gone."

She glanced out the window as they drove along at a break in the forest revealing a wide-open stretch of flat mossy land.

"What I heard is they ain't found hide nor hair of those tourists."

The mention of hides provided Erin with a perfect picture of Carol Walton's mangled body. The rest of the faces of her party flashed before her. Her stomach gave an unexpected and violent pitch, and she had to cover her mouth with her hand.

"That's odd," said Dalton as he gave Erin's arm

a squeeze. She needed to get hold of herself before she gave them away.

Dalton frowned, his look concerned, before he shifted his attention back to the driver, the possible threat.

"It's all been in the papers." The driver frowned. "Course you wouldn't see them out here, I suppose."

Lulu settled back to the man's crowded lap, the wheel just missing the top of her tawny hide.

"That's why I picked you both up. Something terrible is going on up here. I'm Percy, by the way."

Dalton nodded and gave over their real names.

"A pleasure," said Percy. His smile dropped away as he saw something before them. "Oh, okay, they're still here."

Dalton's gaze flicked away, and Erin looked through the dusty windshield.

Before them was a roadblock consisting of two DEC vehicles. One was an SUV and the other a pickup truck parked at such an angle that approaching drivers would have to go around them. This was impossible on the northern side because of the bog. The open stretch might look like a meadow with brush and flowers and even clumps of tall cotton grass, but there were no meadows in these woods. Any cleared space was intentionally cleared by men, or it was clear because it was impossible for trees to grow there. That was the case here for, though the ground looked solid, it was in fact a thick well-adapted spongy mat of living sphagnum, a moss that knit together like raw wool. This bog was famous for both its size and proximity to the road. Hikers venturing onto the moss would quickly find the ground lower and themselves in water up to their ankles. Below was a secret lake.

She knew this because she was scheduled to take a canoeing trip on this very bog. Canoes carrying passengers were heavy enough to sink the moss below their keel so the party could glide along over the bog that sprang back in place after their passing.

Erin looked out at the tuffs where the thick brush was actually cranberry bushes whose blossoms had given way to tight green berries. There were orchids and carnivorous pitcher plants, as well.

"Erin?" She glanced to Dalton. "Percy says we need to show our ID."

"Oh." She turned to look out the back window. "Mine is still in my pack."

She wondered if these were really DEC rangers or CIA agents in disguise. She couldn't ask Dalton, of course, so she just watched as a ranger stepped out from the truck and held up a hand for them to halt.

Percy laughed. "Think the truck in the road is all the stop sign I need."

The ranger wore the correct uniform and utility belt that included a gun. Many of the rangers here were tasked with law enforcement, so that was not all that odd. But the sight made her uncomfortable.

"Where's the other driver?" asked Dalton.

The ranger approached Percy's side of the truck.

Dalton opened his door and had one leg out when the ranger reached Percy.

"Hello again," Percy said.

The ranger dipped to look into the vehicle and then drew his pistol and fired.

Chapter Sixteen

The pistol shot exploded so close to Erin's head that afterward she could hear only a high-pitched buzz. She gasped like a trout suddenly out of water. Percy slumped over the wheel. Her entire body went stiff with terror and sweat popped out all over her body.

Dalton wrenched her from the truck and down to the ground. His service weapon was out and he aimed forward toward the two vehicles, firing three quick shots.

Erin clamped her hands over her ears and squatted beside him, her back against the truck bed. The other ranger fell sideways in front of the truck.

Dalton rose, arms extended to quickly check through the open door to the place where the first man had been, ready to fire through the truck and past Percy. An instant later he dropped down beside her.

"He took the keys," he said.

Her ears still buzzed and his voice seemed distorted. Something moved in the truck and Dalton aimed.

"Wait!" she shouted.

Lulu leaped down from the cab, her coat spattered with Percy's blood. The dog disappeared beneath the truck.

"Where did he go?" she asked, referring to the shooter.

The road was now silent except for Lulu's labored, wheezing breath. Erin dropped to her belly to check the dog and saw the shooter's feet as he rounded the back of the truck.

She tugged at Dalton's sleeve and pointed. He nodded, motioning her under the vehicle. She rolled beneath the truck bed as Dalton dropped to his stomach and fired two shots.

There was a scream and the shooter collapsed to one knee as blood dripped from his foot. Dalton shot him again. Two shots. One in the knee. The other in his hand. The shooter dropped his gun and howled, scrambling back. Then he vanished from sight.

"No shot," said Dalton to himself as his target disappeared.

Erin remembered belatedly that she also had a pistol. She drew it now, holding the muzzle up and hoping she didn't shoot herself in the face. A pounding came from above her head.

Gunfire sent shafts of sunlight beaming through the new holes in the pickup's truck bed.

"We have to get to those vehicles," he said.

"My pack?"

"Leave it."

Dalton tugged her up and pushed her before him. She ran toward the SUV, dancing sideways to avoid the still body sprawled in the road. When she reached the SUV, she peered inside.

"No keys," she said.

Dalton had paused to check the corpse of the downed attacker, rummaging in his pants pockets. An engine revved.

Somehow the shooter had reached the cab with two bullets in his legs and one in his hand. Percy's body lay crumpled in the road beside his truck, and the wounded shooter was throwing the truck into gear.

Dalton made it to her as the truck raced forward. They dove from the road as the driver plowed into the SUV where she had stood. The SUV spun off the road toward them as the truck raced by. She fell to her stomach and slid as the SUV bounced down the embankment in front of them and rolled to its side.

"Where the hell is our backup?" he growled.

The pickup sped past and then turned around.

"He's coming back," said Erin.

Dalton lifted his weapon and fired continuously, every few seconds, with well-timed intervals, as the ranger smashed into the second truck pushing it along the road before him. The driver used Percy's vehicle to sweep the last useful getaway truck into the opposite ditch, where it tipped, engine down and back wheels clear off the ground.

"They did a good job grading this road," said

Erin. The high ground was dry and out of the bog, even after that heavy rain.

"We have zero cover," he said.

"But he lost his weapon," she reminded.

"That truck is two tons of weapon."

Lulu sat on Erin's right foot and glanced up at her. Something niggled in her mind. Two tons of weapon. The idea sprang up like a mushroom after a rain.

"Do you think he has another gun?" she asked, watching him back up.

"If he did, he'd be shooting at us." Dalton removed his empty clip and pushed the spare into place in the pistol's handle.

"You want to keep shooting at him?"

"Unless you have a better idea. We can use the culvert for cover."

"He'll just run us down."

He looked around. "We need to get to the SUV. Use it for cover."

"He can just hit that again."

He gave her an exasperated look. "What do you want to do?"

Their attacker spun Percy's truck back to the road and put it in Reverse.

"He's getting a running start," said Dalton, more to himself than to her.

"We could go out on the bog," she said, pointing.

He glanced at the open area broken only by tufts of grass and clumps of brush. "No cover."

"We won't need it. It's a bog."

He shook his head, not comprehending. "Here he comes."

"That moss is floating on a lake like a carpet or a giant lily pad. He can't drive on it because it's not solid ground."

Dalton turned his head, focusing on the bog now. "Can we run on it?"

"Yes, but we'll get wet. Sink a foot or so. It's spongy, like running on foam rubber and—"

He cut her off. "Okay. Okay. Go!"

She lifted Lulu off her foot and into her arms, then darted down the hill past the SUV. The tail section of the vehicle had already sunk into the moss, which accommodated the weight by moving out of the way.

Running out on the sweet-smelling, soggy sphagnum moss was like running on a field of wet loofah sponges, a rare experience that she would have enjoyed in other circumstances. The plant that most people only saw in wreaths and at the base of floral arrangements was a living sponge and just as easy to run upon.

Dalton swore as he stumbled and tipped forward. The bog absorbed his fall like a living crash pad, soaking his front in six inches of clear water. He scrambled to his feet, now standing in twelve inches of water as she raced ahead of him. She'd been on this bog before, looking for native orchids to show her expedition, and knew the best way was high steps and a little bounce. Her experience allowed her to get well out in front of him. Lulu whined in her arms and scrambled to reach her shoulder. Once there the little dog perched, looking back at the truck that was no doubt in pursuit.

"Erin?" Dalton paused, glancing behind him. They had made it some forty feet out on the bog.

Not far enough, she feared, seeing the pickup gaining speed in what she thought might be preparation for a jump from the road, some five feet above them, and onto the bog.

If he landed near them, the truck would sink down with the moss and take them with it. And the moss would tear... She had a dreadful premonition of what could happen to them. Stories told of early settlers rose in her memory. Entire mule teams vanishing with wagons and all. Swallowed up in an instant as the sphagnum moss rent like fabric, dropping men, animals and wagons through the spongy layer that instantly sprang back into place above them. Leaving them beneath the two feet of moss and as trapped as anyone who had ever been swept beneath ice by the water's current.

Her heart raced as she looked around for something to anchor them should the moss tear, keep them on the right side of the sphagnum mat, even if they temporarily sank.

"Grab the cranberry bushes and don't let go!" she yelled to Dalton.

She dove, using her one arm to grip Lulu and the other to latch onto the wrist-sized trunk of a hearty bush covered in tight green berries.

Dalton did not ask questions or try to take control. He just followed suit, landing beside her. Their combined weight sank them in eighteen inches of cold clear water. She lifted her head to breathe and looked back.

The truck was airborne. Lulu struggled, her body underwater. Erin held on.

The impact of the truck rolled under them like a wave. The vehicle landed upright, several yards away. Instead of speeding along the open field, it stopped dead as the tires turned uselessly and the motor revved.

The driver's hand went straight up as the moss sank instantly to the windows under the two tons of weight. She heard the wail and saw the brilliant red blood streaming down his shooting arm from his wounded hand. The moss yielded without a sound, the gash tipping the truck engine down before the vehicle vanished. The scream cut short as the moss sprang back into position, grass, plants and bushes appearing just as they had been, leaving no sign of the horror that must be playing out beneath them.

Erin rolled to her back and Lulu dog-paddled away, her stumpy front legs thrashing until she reached a clump of grass that barely moved under her slight weight. There Lulu sat on a pitcher plant, panting.

Dalton lifted a hand to his forehead.

"Remind me to never cross you," he said. He sat

up in the water that reached his hips, staring back at the empty bog. "It's like it never happened."

He was soaking wet, with bits of pale yellow-green moss sticking to his clothing.

"Why aren't there any helicopters or CIA agents charging from the trees?" Erin asked.

He glanced around. "Great question."

"You know what I think?"

"What?" He had one hand pressed to his forehead as he continued to look back at the tranquil expanse, disbelieving.

"They're dangling us like a worm on a hook," she said. "Doesn't matter what happens to the worm as long as you catch the fish."

"Only both our fish are gone."

She nodded. "We should get off this bog."

"I'll say."

"It's a protected habitat. I don't want to damage it any more than necessary."

"You're worried about the swamp?"

"Bog. It's a completely different ecosystem from a wetland. I'm scheduled to lead expeditions on this very site later in the week."

"Well, if I'd known that, I wouldn't have let you come up here." He tucked his gun into a pocket that was still underwater and shook his head in bewilderment. "And you think *my* job is dangerous?"

Chapter Seventeen

"They wanted one alive," said Erin to Dalton as they stood on the road staring out at the bog. They were soaking wet and the breeze chilled him, but not as much as that sphagnum moss.

"You can't even see the tear. Nothing." Dalton shook his head. "It's the most terrifying thing I've ever seen." He glanced her way. "You canoe on that?"

"Walk, too. It's safe."

"Yeah, right. You'll never convince me of that."

She hiked Lulu up higher on her chest and scratched behind the dog's ear. "Now what?"

"The way I see it," Dalton said, "we can wait for the Feds to come and perform their catch and release. Try to capture another member of this terrorist outfit, preferably without getting killed, or we can get out of here and try to make it to someplace safe."

"Nowhere is safe as long as they think we have the vials."

"You're right, and I have a feeling Siming's Army will not take our word for it that it's gone."

"And we have no proof that the CIA took it from us."

"Or that we even met with them." He turned to her. "What do you think?"

Her brows lifted, and she stopped stroking the trembling dog. He wanted to take her in his arms and hold her, tell her that they'd get out of this. But he was no longer sure. Bringing her back out here now seemed the stupidest play imaginable. The CIA didn't have their back. His fanny was swinging out here in the breeze, and he'd dragged her with him.

The uncomfortable distance that had yawned between them, the one he had hoped to close, seemed to have torn open again.

"You're asking me what I think?" She didn't have to look so astonished.

"Yeah," he said, unable to keep the terseness from his tone. "I'm asking."

"I think we shouldn't have trusted those agents. I think we now have nothing to bargain with."

"Easy to catch us whichever way we go," he said. "And it's anyone's guess who will show up first."

"I hope it's not someone like Percy. That poor man."

Lulu licked under Erin's chin, the pink tongue curling up his wife's jaw.

"Oh, you poor thing."

"You keeping her, too?" asked Dalton, already knowing the answer.

"I'm not leaving her on a bog."

"Those pitcher plants might eat her," he said,

referring to the cylindrical plants that held a sweet water designed to lure and drown insects. She'd told him about them once before. Not as flashy as the Venus flytrap, but just as deadly.

She didn't laugh at his joke. Lulu was tiny but not small enough to succumb to carnivorous plants. And not big enough to keep up on a hike, either.

Erin scratched under Lulu's chin. "Not a chance. Right, Lulu?"

The soft and sympathetic voice caused a sharp pang of regret. Not that he wanted her to speak to him this way; still he could imagine her, cooing and fussing over a baby. Their baby. But first they had to get out of this mess alive.

"I'm going to check the other one for keys." He thumbed back at the corpse sprawled in the road. Erin followed him and then turned to look at the sky.

"You think they're up there watching?" she asked, using her hand as a visor.

"Definitely."

Erin lifted her hand from her eyes and presented her middle finger to the sky.

Dalton laughed. "Feel better?"

She gave him a half smile as if that were all she could spare. He went back to searching the pockets of the dead man. His diligence was rewarded. The guy kept his keys in his front shirt pocket, which was why he'd missed them before.

He stood and tossed the keys a few inches, catching them again. Then he looked at the pickup truck, engine down and back wheels off the ground. The vehicle was diagonally across from the SUV, which lay on its side at the bottom of the opposite incline. Neither one of them was getting them out of here.

Lulu stood at the road alone. Erin had disappeared. His heart gave a jolt as he glanced to the bog. But Lulu was on the opposite side of the road, panting.

He headed that way at a run. Once he reached the chubby pug, he found his wife. Her head popped up out of the door of the cap that covered the truck bed. Because of the odd angle, the truck sat nearly vertical and the rear door opened out like a mailbox.

"Erin?"

She had something in her hand. "Did you find the keys?"

"Got them." He lifted the chain.

"Try the fob," she said, and scrambled out, sitting on the closed tailgate, legs dangling.

He hit the unlock button and the truck chimed.

He glanced down the bank and saw the truck sat nose down on the hill with the front tires rooting on the incline and the grille buried in the ground beyond.

Erin tossed something from the truck. She dragged a length of chain from within. It rattled over the closed tailgate, extending to the ground. She looped the hook, at the end, around the ball-mount trailer hitch beneath the bumper.

"How did you even get up there?" he asked, looking to the truck's tailgate now above his head.

"Lulu boosted me."

He chuckled and looked at the dog, who sat on one hip, tail between her legs and eyes closed in the bright sunlight.

Meanwhile, Erin scrambled like a monkey over the top of the truck and slid down the cap roof to the cab and then dropped to the ground.

"Keys?" she asked, and he tossed them down.

Erin disappeared into the cab and emerged a moment later.

"They're in the ignition and the truck is in neutral."

Dalton lifted the chain and gazed at the truck. Whatever she had in mind, he knew they would not be able to tug this truck up that incline.

She appeared up the hill a moment later.

"Riding beats walking when you are in a hurry," she said.

"How you planning to get that truck back on the road?"

She grinned. "The SUV has a winch on the front. "I figure we attach the two and see which one makes it up the incline and to the road first."

He pressed his lips together and nodded. "Let's go."

The chain reached across the road and the winch cable easily reached the chain.

"We don't have the keys for that SUV," reminded Dalton.

"City boy," she said. "This winch is electric. You

don't need to turn on the vehicle to run it. Step back now. Where's Lulu?"

He lifted the dog and moved up the bank. She proceeded to flip a lever and then flicked a toggle switch.

"Holler when the truck is on the road."

The cable began to move, stretching taut. There was a hesitation as the cable vibrated, and then the SUV dragged on its side, inching to the hill below the road. The whine of the winch was momentarily obscured by the scrape of gravel and rock beneath metal. Once the SUV reached the incline it paused as the cable continued to reel.

Dalton glanced across the road, following the cable to the upended pickup and saw it teeter. The back tires thumped down to the road and then the truck rolled with slow inertia up the hill. Since the SUV was lighter than the truck and not anchored, it was dragged up the incline as the truck crept along. By the time the pickup was on the road, the SUV was nearly up the hill.

"Good," he shouted.

The winch motor cut and the whining ceased. Erin instructed him to start the truck and drive it toward the SUV until the chain dropped so she could release the winch safely. He did and the SUV slipped back down the hill as he rolled forward. But the winched vehicle came to a stop before he left the road. Erin scrambled up the embankment and then released the winch cable, tossing it back into the culvert. She gathered the chain and threw it into the truck bed. A moment later she climbed into the truck. Lulu was ecstatic to see her, wiggling and wagging and then throwing herself to her back.

"Jet is going to eat that dog," he predicted.

She gathered up the little tan lapdog into her arms. "Where to?"

"That way has no outlet, just a loop to the gun club that will bring you back here," he reminded her.

"Right. Minerva it is."

He put the truck in motion. "You still have your pistol?"

She patted her jacket pocket. He flicked on the heater, hoping the air would help dry his clothing and warm them.

"I hate bogs," he mumbled.

She laughed and settled Lulu on her lap. Then she clicked her seat belt across her middle.

"Think we can make it to your partner in North Creek?"

"I doubt it. But that's where I'm heading."

She peered out the open window, gazing at the blue sky.

"They still up there?"

"Probably."

They did not even slow down in the town of Minerva and he was surprised that no one stopped them.

"How many people do you think are up here with Siming's Army?" she asked as they cruised past a gas station that advertised firewood and propane.

"Six fewer now," he said. "But I don't know. That could be all of them in one sleeper cell."

"Our attackers weren't in uniform," she said. "But the truck is DEC."

Erin busied herself searching the glove box. She found a bag of trail mix, the kind with chocolate mingled in with the nuts and raisins. She offered it open to him and continued her exploration while he munched.

"Nothing but the paperwork and some tools." She pocketed the universal multi-tool. Just as well, as she clearly knew how to use one better than he would.

He pulled into a KOA and drew up to the office. He handed back the half-empty bag and she lifted it, pouring some of the contents into her mouth and then offering Lulu a peanut.

"I need to make a phone call," he said.

She nodded and held Lulu, who tried to follow him out of the vehicle. Dalton used the office pay phone to call Henry Larson, who had not left the area, despite not being allowed to see him or, perhaps, because of it. The two made arrangements on how and where to meet, and then Dalton returned to Erin.

"Let me guess," she said. "You called Henry."

"I did."

"NYPD to the rescue," she said.

"I get it. You don't like Henry." He set them back in motion, pulling out of the campground's lot.

"True."

"Because when I'm with him, I'm not with you?"

"Because he thinks strip clubs are an acceptable form of entertainment and because he has a different girlfriend every time he comes to a party. Where does he get them all?"

Dalton wisely did not answer, but Erin's eyebrows rose, making the connection.

"So he's dating strippers?"

"They weren't *all* strippers."

"Oh, that makes me feel so much better."

"I don't want to fight."

"We aren't fighting," she said, as she always did. But they were.

"Do you know why I came up here after you?" he asked.

"To convince me to come home or at least not to ask for a trial separation."

"True. And because I don't want to become like Henry. I wanted to try, to keep trying."

This revelation had an effect that was the opposite of what Dalton had intended. Erin blew through her nostrils and turned her head to stare out the window at the homes that had cut grassy plots out of the surrounding woodland. They were off parkland, he realized.

Dalton tried again. "Henry is a good guy. A solid guy. He loves his kids. He's a good father, but he has nothing but terrible things to say about his wife. He thinks that she's the reason for him losing his house and only seeing his kids on weekends. All his problems start and end with his ex."

She turned to stare out the front window. Listening, her face revealing nothing.

"I know how many cops are divorced. The statistics. I know the stats on drinking and drug abuse. It's a tough job. Stressful."

"On families, too," she said in a voice that seemed faraway.

"But I never thought that would be me. Be us. We were rock solid. I came home every night I wasn't working. I shared what I could instead of keeping it bottled up inside. Now I think that might have been a mistake. Telling you—I mean, because it frightened you. Some of the guys said I was stupid, letting you know the risks we take. The close calls. That this was the reason they didn't share work stories at home. Kids don't need to hear it and wives freak."

"I never freaked."

"You did. You left me and came here."

"Not because I was listening but because you weren't."

"I listened. But this is who I am. I'm a protector at heart. I live to get those criminals off the streets. To stop them before they can hurt anyone and see they never get the chance to try again."

"Which is why people are still shooting at us."

"Erin, I thought you agreed."

"That was before they ditched us. We have no backup or none that I have seen. I understand why we are here and I accept that what you do is important. I just can't live like this anymore."

"Erin. Please."

"I'm scared," she admitted.

She had good reason. The way this was heading, saving their marriage might be the least of their problems.

"We'll get through this."

She shook her head. "If we do, what then?"

"You come home. We work this out."

She stared vacantly at her scabby knees and offered no reassurance.

He extended his hand but, instead of squeezing it back, she just stared at it. He rested it on her leg, feeling the warm skin and firm muscle beneath. After a millennium, she moved her hand from the dog and covered his.

It was a start. Or he hoped it was.

"Are we going to get out of this?" she asked.

He set his jaw and nodded. "Yes, ma'am, we surely are."

"That just wishful thinking? Telling me what you think I need to hear."

He shook his head. "I can't believe there are this many of them. Erin, the woods are crawling with these terrorists. And I don't understand why we haven't already been picked up and brought back in."

"Because we didn't get a member of Siming's Army, not a living one anyway."

He shook his head again. Something was wrong. The Feds had not held up their end of the bargain, and that meant the deal was off. All men for themselves. He needed to look after his own and get Erin to safety.

Lulu shifted position, groaned and lay down on Erin's lap.

"Do you think she knows what happened to Percy?"

"No."

"Dogs grieve the loss of their owners, you know."

"I suppose." But Lulu's bulging eyes made her look more hungry than grief stricken.

"Are you regretting coming out here?" he asked.

She stared straight ahead, and he had the feeling something was really wrong. Mostly because she wasn't angry and she had a right to be. He'd trusted the system and they'd been dumped in a bog as reward. Finally, she spoke, and her voice was flat calm as the eye of a hurricane.

"I would have preferred that they put out an APB that we'd been picked up and processed and released, so everyone would know we don't have that darn black case."

She cut a sidelong glance at him and then rested a trembling hand on Lulu's back. She stroked the resting dog, seeming to draw comfort from the tiny creature.

That other woman, the Homeland Security agent, would not have known to take them out on the bog, and he very much doubted that Hockings knew how to use a winch. Maybe she could have shot and killed that second man. But he'd never know. He was happy to stay with the one who had brought him to the dance. But was she happy about it?

They reached an actual intersection and a stop sign. The dirt road ended against NY 28 and he turned south, away from Minerva and toward North Creek. The southern route flanked the Hudson on the opposite side from where they had walked yesterday over the trestle and all the way to North River. They covered the four miles in less than five minutes and crossed the river. Groups of rafters drifted by on the calm section before the upcoming set of rapids. Next, they journeyed through North River, with its white-water rafting outfits perched directly across the road from the launching sites.

Dalton didn't slow but continued toward North Creek. Henry was waiting.

"Did you speak to the CIA guys?" she asked.

"Yeah. They took the drive and samples."

"Tillman was okay. Seemed nice enough but that other one. What was his name, Danielson?" she asked.

"No, that's not it. First name was Cliff, I think. Or Clint."

"I don't think it was Clint. I can't even remember what he looked like." She rubbed her chin, thinking.

"There were a lot of federal agents. Two from the

FBI. Agent Shaffer, also CIA and the Homeland Security agents."

Why had he mentioned them? Now she'd be thinking of Hockings again.

"Were you questioned by the guy? Forester?" she asked.

"Foster, Lawrence," he said. He thought of the agent he had met in the men's room realizing then that the guy had said he'd join him in interrogation but never showed "I met him, but we didn't have a formal interview. You?"

"Yes. He gave me the creeps."

"Worse than Clint or Cliff?"

"Different. He was the only one who showed up alone. After the other agents left. I felt, not threatened, but cornered, I guess. He was with me until just before you arrived. He didn't ask the same things as the CIA men. He wanted to know about the pilot. Where he was and how he died. What happened to the woman who owned the dog and where we had been last night. He was the only one who asked about the contents of what we carried."

"They have the contents. Why ask you?"

"Maybe that's what bothered me. He also was the first to ask where we had been heading and which of your colleagues you had contacted."

Dalton's radar popped on and he scowled. "Where we were heading? Did you tell him about Henry?"

"Of course."

Dalton stepped on the gas.

Erin sat forward, grabbing the overhead hand grip. "What? What's wrong?"

Lulu startled awake as she nearly fell off Erin's lap to the floor mats.

"You see his ID?"

"I... I don't remember. I didn't see Hockings's ID. I know that."

"What if Foster is not DHS?" he asked.

"Then he wouldn't have been in the troopers' headquarters."

That wasn't necessarily true. All they had to do was to get someone to buzz them in and mingle with people in the building. It was alphabet soup in there.

"If he was legit, then he'd know that the CIA recovered the flash drive and vials."

"So?" she asked.

"He'd also know we aren't carrying anything. No reason to attack us back there."

That was true, unless their attackers had not gotten word from him or it was a different cell.

"But he asked about Henry?"

"Yes. All he knew was that Henry was NYPD SWAT. Not his name, even." She shook her head. "But Henry doesn't have anything they want."

"Neither do we, but those men by the bog still tried to kill us."

She didn't argue with that, just held on as he

flew along the highway passing a Subaru with bikes fixed to the back end and a family SUV with canoes strapped to the roof racks.

Chapter Eighteen

"I don't understand why we didn't have any backup out there," she said.

"That's just one of my questions," said Dalton.

They tore into the parking area of a chain hotel. Dalton leaped out of the truck and charged through lobby doors that barely had time to whisk open. Erin lowered the windows and told Lulu to stay. Then she followed him inside in time to see him leaning over the desk of the petite receptionist dressed in a polyester blazer with a gold-toned name tag.

"I can't tell you his room number." She lifted the phone. "But I can call his room for you."

Dalton flashed his shield to the receptionist. The wallet was soggy and much worse for wear, but the receptionist's reaction was instant. Her fingers started tapping on the keys.

"He's in 116. First floor, right down that hallway."

"Call 911. Tell them NYC detective Dalton Stevens requests backup for possible B and E."

"Yes, sir."

He pointed at Erin. "Stay here."

"Like hell," she said.

She'd seen enough cop shows to know how to enter a room with a gun. And if Rylee Hockings could do it, she could, too.

Dalton dashed down the hall toward his colleague's room and she followed at a run. When he reached the door, he motioned her to halt, and he stood to the side to try the handle. The door was locked. Then he lifted one booted foot and kicked in the flimsy hotel room door.

He entered with pistol raised and the grip cradled in his opposite hand. Erin watched him disappear and then heard nothing.

She crept farther down the hall and made out her husband's voice.

"Larson?"

Did he see his friend or was he just looking?

There was no reply. Erin peeked around the doorjamb and saw Henry Larson sprawled on the floor, his hands secured behind his back. Dalton squatted at his side.

"Is he dead?" she asked.

Before he could answer, Dalton rose to face her and his eyes went wild. He reached and took two steps toward her. Then she felt it, the hand clutching her jacket from behind, dragging her off her feet, across the hall and into the opposite hotel room. The fabric choked her, sending her hand reflexively to her throat.

Dalton reached the hallway as her captor kicked the door to the opposite hotel room closed and threw the bolt. The impact of Dalton's body against the door vibrated through the soles of her kicking feet.

On the second attempt Dalton crashed through the door. His gun was up and raised as he advanced with measured steps.

"Far enough," said her captor. She felt the hard pressure of the pistol pushing into her temple.

Dalton paused, as if playing some deadly game of freeze tag, but his weapon remained up and pointed at her captor.

"Foster, isn't it?" asked her husband.

"For now," said the man who had spoken to her in the darn troopers' headquarters just prior to Dalton's arrival with the three federal agents, Hockings, Tillman and Shaffer. He had identified himself as Lawrence Foster, an agent with the Department of Homeland Security.

"Lower your weapon or I kill your wife." He said it as a cashier might tell you to hold on while they print your receipt. The effect was chilling. The man was cold-blooded as a garter snake.

Dalton said nothing but his eyes were on her attacker. The gun barrel moved to her eye socket.

"All right. It's down," said Dalton. "What do you want?"

"To interrogate the two remaining witnesses. Find out how much they know about us."

"We don't have the package. It's with the agents at the troopers'—"

Foster cut him off. "I know that. Which is why I blew that building. That virus is now airborne. Anybody sifting through the ashes has a great chance of contracting our little superbug, and the vaccine, well, that doesn't go airborne." He made a *tsking* sound with his tongue on the roof of his mouth.

Was it true? Was that why there was no backup? Were they all dead?

The chill shook her. Was it really just her husband and her and this madman?

"Out," said Foster.

She didn't know where they were going and, right this second, she didn't care. What she did care about was seeing that Dalton did not get shot by some maniac terrorist. She and her husband were going to take Lulu and Jet home to Yonkers and give them a home. Dalton was going to make good on his promise to become a supervisor, and she was going to see that they spent every free minute trying to start that family.

If Foster didn't shoot her and her husband first.

What would Dalton do?

Something heavy pressed against her side. The pistol, the small one that she'd carried since Jet's captor tried to kill them. Her hand slipped inside her jacket pocket and she gripped the weapon. Her thumb flicked off the safety. He marched her forward. Sweat ran behind her ears and into her hair. It rolled between her breasts and down the long channel of her spine.

Dalton retreated to the hallway as they reached his discarded weapon. The man stooped and his pistol dropped toward her neck. He motioned with the gun to the floor.

"Pick that up," he ordered her. "Barrel first."

Erin slipped the pistol from her pocket and met Dalton's gaze. She'd never seen him afraid before. But that was what she saw now. Stone-cold terror in the hardening of his jaw and the hands extending reflexively toward her.

DALTON HAD STOPPED backing up when he saw Erin's hand moving in her pocket. His breath caught. His jaw locked and he saw stars.

No. No. No.

He'd only set down his gun to keep Foster from killing Erin. But she had other plans, as always.

Had she remembered to flick off the safety of her weapon? His gaze dropped for just an instant to the small silver pistol in her hand, but it was enough.

Foster's eyes narrowed on him and he lifted the handgun that was now pointing across Erin's chest.

Dalton took a step forward. Foster hesitated as if deciding whether to aim at Erin or back at him. Erin lifted the gun under her opposite armpit and fired back at Foster hitting him in the chest. He released her, staggering backward, still aiming at them. Dalton made a grab for Erin and missed.

Erin spun to face Foster and stepped between them as Foster fired a single shot.

Chapter Nineteen

Every hair on Dalton's body lifted and his heart stuttered before exploding into a frantic pounding. Erin spun, staring at Dalton's shocked expression as Foster aimed at him. But he'd reached him now and grabbed Foster's wrist, then used his opposite hand to break Foster's elbow as he retrieved the man's pistol from his limp hand.

Dalton pointed his attacker's pistol at Foster, but his gaze flicked from his target to Erin, who sank to her knees, gasping. In that moment, Foster ducked past the doorjamb and out of sight.

The small pistol dropped to the carpet as his wife lifted her hand to her neck, pale fingers clamping down as blood welled from beneath her palm.

His head swam and he shook it in a vain attempt to wake from this nightmare. Erin stared at him, her eyes wide and round, showing the whites all about her brown irises.

"Erin. No," he whispered to himself as the truth

ricocheted through him like the bullet that had struck her.

Erin was bleeding.

She toppled, her hand dropping away from her neck, allowing blood to pour out of her body, staining the carpet.

A wild shrieking came from the man darting down the hall to the lobby, his ruined arm flailing, his elbow jutting out at an odd angle. It took a moment for Dalton to realize that part of the screaming was the wail of approaching sirens. Help arriving too late.

Dalton let his suspect run as he dropped to his knees beside his wife. He gathered her limp body in his arms. She was going to die, leaving him after all but not in the way she had planned.

He tore back the jacket from her neck and saw the bullet hole at the point where her long neck gave way to her shoulder. A gentle probing told him that the collarbone was intact, and from the way the blood exited the wound he was certain that the bullet had not struck her carotid artery because there was no spraying of blood. But it had hit some blood vessel because the hole was a deep bubbling well of red.

She was going to leave him like his men back in Afghanistan. Like his partner, Chris Wirimer. Why was he still here when everyone he tried to protect...

"Dalton?" Her voice was weak, but her gaze fixed him steadily. "You okay?"

She was worried about him. Always. And suddenly he understood. This was exactly what she had feared, only their roles had reversed. How many times had she imagined him bleeding out at some crime scene?

This was what he'd done to her, year after year, because he couldn't stand being the one who made it out.

His broad hand clamped over her wound and pressed hard. He would not let her bleed out on the hallway like some…some…hero, he realized. She'd saved his life, possibly Henry Larson's life as well, if he wasn't already dead.

"I'm here. Help is coming. Hold on, Erin."

"Did he shoot you?" she asked.

"No."

She closed her eyes then, and relaxed against him.

"Thank God," she whispered.

Dalton felt the tightening in his throat, the burning as his eyes watered, vision swimming.

Then he started screaming for help. Doors cracked open as people crept cautiously out of their rooms.

"Bring help," he shouted. "Get her help!"

She had wanted to leave that package behind. Put it on a red T-shirt with a note, she had suggested. But he had to bring it along.

If Foster could be believed, he'd destroyed it anyway, and by bringing it out of the woods, possibly Dalton had jeopardized who knew how many lives, begun some Siming's pandemic for them. But now, the only life he cared about was Erin's.

He stroked her damp hair and stared down the hall until, at last, the EMTs arrived, charging toward him in navy blue uniforms, their bulky bags flopping against their thighs.

"Hang on, Erin. Don't you leave me."

THEY LET DALTON ride in the first ambulance with Erin but did not let him into the operating wing. He was directed to a waiting area as Erin disappeared down a long corridor, followed by his partner, Henry Larson, on a second gurney. The waiting room had wooden chairs with mauve cushions set in a U-shape around three coffee tables holding a smattering of torn magazines and discarded paper coffee cups. There were two other men already there, and he was surprised to find both CIA agent Jerome Shaffer and FBI agent Nolen Bersen waiting.

"So it's true then," he said. "Troopers' headquarters is gone?"

Bersen nodded. "Agent Heller suffered injuries. He is in surgery now."

"So is Erin. Gunshot wound to her neck."

Shaffer stood and placed a hand on Dalton's shoulder. "Sorry to hear that."

"Anyone else hurt?" asked Dalton.

"Mostly minor injuries. The troopers have a K-9 dog. Former marine, and he found the explosives. They were clearing the building when it went off. Heller was hit by part of the ceiling. He's got a spine injury."

"What about the…" Dalton looked around. "What we brought in?"

"Long gone. Shaffer and Gabriel had it out of the station well before the blast. It's safe, Stevens."

Why didn't that make him feel any better?

"She's in there because of me."

"This isn't your fault, Dalton."

"I agreed to go back out there. I let her come along. Of course, it's my fault."

"I understand you're upset. With good reason. Your wife is injured and your colleague, Detective Larson, suffered head trauma in an attack," said Shaffer.

"Yeah, they just brought him in with her."

"What happened?"

Dalton's eyes widened as he realized that Shaffer didn't know about the impostor and therefore the agent from Siming's Army was getting away. "At the troopers' headquarters there was a man. We both met him. Said he was DHS, name was Lawrence Foster."

"Foster?" asked Shaffer. "I don't know him."

Dalton explained, finishing with, "He shot Erin. Don't let him get away."

Both men lifted their phones.

"So there is no Lawrence Foster of DHS?"

Shaffer lifted the phone from his mouth, pointing the bottom toward the ceiling. "No."

"Then how did he get into trooper headquarters?"

"I'll be checking that."

"What about the other one, Rylee Hockings?"

"She's DHS. On her way back to her offices in Glens Falls."

While Dalton paced, Shaffer and Bersen made calls.

He didn't realize that Agent Shaffer was speaking to him until he touched Dalton's shoulder.

"We got him."

"Who?" He'd been so lost in thought and worry that it took a moment to come back to his surroundings. Dalton was in the hallway now, standing on the wide tiles before the doors that read No Admittance.

"Lawrence Foster, or the man claiming to be Foster. Troopers caught him trying to board an Amtrak train in Glens Falls. Arm injury made him easy to spot."

"Sweating like a marathon runner," added Bersen.

"He had the proper ID for DHS. Either real or a very convincing fake."

Dalton felt none of the elation that usually accompanied a collar. He didn't care. Not unless they'd let him see him alone so he could settle up. And he knew that would never happen.

How many victims had asked him for that same thing?

"He alive?" Dalton asked, his voice mechanical.

"Yes, in custody. His real name is Vincent Eulich. He's a physicist, college professor in Schenectady with a bomb-making hobby."

"We already have agents at his home and office. But we have to go slow. Already found one IED," said Bersen, referring to the improvised explosive devices most commonly in use in the Middle East.

A man in blue scrubs emerged from the swinging doors and all conversation ceased.

"Anyone out here waiting for word on Henry Larson?"

"I'm in his department," said Dalton. And Henry was his best friend.

"Any direct family?" asked the surgeon.

"Not here. He's got an ex-wife and two kids."

The surgeon pulled a face.

"I'm Dr. Howard. Your colleague has suffered a spine fracture in three places. The rest is cuts and bruises and a mild concussion as a result of a head injury. The back injury is most serious. But the pressure is off the spinal cord and I've repaired a herniated disk. His prognosis is good. Barring complications, I'd say he'll be able to use his legs again after some physical therapy."

That news hit Dalton in the stomach like a mule kick.

"Walk? The man's a former Army Ranger. He bikes all over Westchester and runs Ironman contests."

The surgeon shook his head. "I doubt he'll be doing any of those things again. He'll need a spinal fusion once the swelling is down."

"Fusion?" Removal from active duty, Dalton realized. Just like that.

Dr. Howard nodded. "Got to get back at it."

Dalton grasped his elbow and Howard's expression showed surprise.

"Any word on Erin Stevens? She was shot in the neck?"

"Different surgical team. I'm sure they'll be out to you as soon as they can."

"Anything?" Dalton said, his voice gruff.

"Still in surgery."

He gave Dalton a tight smile and backed through the swinging doors.

Dalton walked slowly to the waiting area and sank into a chair. Bersen and Shaffer took up seats opposite. Dalton folded his hands and bowed his head. He had not done this in some time. Praying felt awkward and uncomfortable. Still he muscled through, asking God's help in saving his wife. When he finished he found both agents regarding him.

"You two waiting on someone?"

"Yes," said Shaffer. "You. And your wife. We need to be sure Siming's Army knows we have the intel they tried and failed to recover and that you two are safe. We've also got two agents outside of the operating room."

"After they know that, you think they'll try to hurt Erin again?"

"They seem determined to kill you both. So we've called some friends from WITSEC."

Dalton straightened at the mention of the witness protection program.

"That's extreme, don't you think?"

"Temporary placement. Until we get this organization shut down."

Dalton sat back in the uncomfortable little chair. They didn't think it was too extreme. What would Erin say? What about him? He had a mom, a dad and stepmother, plus two older sisters. Erin had a brother she rarely saw and a sister who lived on the same block.

His job… He'd have to leave his job and, even after relocation, he would not be able to work in law enforcement again.

A voice came from the edge of the carpet just outside of the waiting area.

"Mr. Stevens? I have an update on your wife."

Chapter Twenty

Erin woke in pain and in the company of strangers. She asked for Dalton and a nurse's blurry face appeared above her. When the nurse didn't understand, Erin tried to pull the mask off her own face. There was a sharp sting on her hip and she sank back into blackness.

The next time she roused, fighting every inch of the way back to consciousness, it was to a room of light and sound. Machines bleated and chimed. Alarms chirped and she squinted against the blinding lights above her.

"What time?" she tried to ask the attendant who checked the fluid bag that hung above her on a metal pole.

"You're doing great, honey," said a female voice.

"What time?" Her voice was the scratch of sandpaper on dry wood.

"It's nearly 9:00 p.m. You're out of recovery and in ICU. Your husband just left. He's a handsome fellow. Needs a shave, though."

"Dalton?"

"That right? I thought you said *Walton*. Anyway. He seems nice. You'll be here tonight and tomorrow. You do okay and you'll get a room. You in trouble, honey?"

"Trouble?" Other than getting shot? she wondered.

"There are two US marshals right outside. I know they aren't for me. So you in trouble?"

"Not anymore." Talking hurt so badly she had to close her eyes.

"You hurting?"

She nodded and immediately regretted it. The nurse used a syringe to add something to her IV line and Erin's body went slack. The pain dissolved like fog in the sun and she slipped away to a place beyond the needs of her body.

"Erin?"

She knew that voice.

"Erin. It's Dalton."

She tried and failed to open her eyes.

"Can you hear me?" He lifted her limp hand. "Squeeze my hand."

She tried, failed and swallowed. The pain was back. Her throat throbbed as if she were a tree trunk and a woodpecker was knocking a hole into her with repeated stabbing blows.

"Your sister, Victoria, is here."

Another voice, female murmuring. Erin tried again to open her eyes, but the deep pain-free well beckoned.

She let go and dropped. Just like rappelling down a cliff, she thought as she glided into blackness.

DALTON DIDN'T SEE the surgeon until the following day. The guy had sent a physician's assistant out to see him in the waiting room yesterday, and his visits during the night had scared him silly. Erin had a bandage the size of a football on her neck. And she was on a ventilator.

Her sister, Vic, had arrived at nine and the physician appeared at bedside during the fifteen minutes they allowed Dalton each hour. Vic had stepped out at the MD's appearance so Dalton could step in.

"The loss of blood resulted in your wife suffering a cardiac arrest. To reduce her energy expenditure, I ordered a drug-induced coma. The medication is keeping her body from using any extra energy, easing the burden on her heart."

"How long will you keep her like this?" asked Dalton.

"Until her blood volume is normal and her bladder is functioning again." He motioned to the empty clear bag hanging from the bed rails. Had her kidney's stopped working?

Panic tightened its grip upon him.

"Days?" asked Dalton.

"Likely we'll wake her up later today. Your wife lost a lot of blood. It can damage organs. We need to be sure everything is working."

"If it's not?"

"One thing at a time."

The next twenty-four hours were the longest of his life. Because of him, his best friend had suffered a spinal injury and his wife was in a coma. As minutes ticked away, Dalton had lots of time to make promises to God and curse his own foolishness. Nothing was as important to him as his friend and his wife. He just hoped that he'd have a chance to tell them both.

ERIN'S EYES POPPED OPEN. It was as if someone had just flicked a switch and brought her to full awake. Tentative movement told her that she had not imagined her injuries.

Four unfamiliar faces peered down at her.

"Mrs. Stevens? How do you feel?"

"Thirsty," she said.

They asked her a series of questions that seemed designed to test her mental acumen. The day, month, who was president? What holiday was next on the calendar, and math problems.

"Is my husband here?"

"He is. And anxious to see you. But a brief visit. Right?" The physician looked to another attendee, who nodded. Brightly colored cartoon illustrations of popular candy bars covered this man's scrubs top.

Three of the gathering wandered out in conversation as the one male attendant remained.

"I'm Will. I'm your nurse today."

"Hi, Will. Um, water?"

"Ice chips for now." He fussed with the IV bag and then disappeared, returning with a plastic cup. "I did one better. Lemon ice. Okay?" He handed it over with a plastic spoon.

Erin discovered that she could not really work her left hand without waking the dragon of burning pain in her shoulder.

Man, it hurt to get shot.

Dalton arrived, hurrying forward and then slowing as he saw her. He looked as bad as she felt.

"Oh, Dalton!" she said.

"Erin?" He got only that out and then he did something she had never seen him do. He wept.

Both hands covered his big, tired face and his shoulders shook. She reached her good hand to him and called his name.

He peered at her beneath his dark brows and raised hands. The circles under his eyes startled and he looked thinner. Then he took her hand and allowed her to draw him to her bed, where he sat awkwardly on the edge.

"You're awake," he said.

She smiled. "They gave me an ice. But I can't manage holding and scooping."

Dalton took over both jobs, offering her wonderful sweet, cold bits of frozen lemon. Nothing had ever tasted so good, though the act of eating and swallowing hurt her neck. She didn't say so but was relieved when Will came to roust Dalton back out. The weariness tugged at her features and pricked at her skin.

"I'll see you soon."

She held her smile until he was out of sight and then groaned.

"Pain?" asked Will.

She nodded and then flinched. Will returned with the pain medication and then the throbbing ache retreated like a receding tide. She breathed a sigh.

"Thanks."

"Your sister is out there. I'll send her in after you take a little nap."

She murmured her acceptance and closed her eyes. What choice did she have? For the rest of that day and through the night, she had short visits with Victoria and Dalton. The following day she felt so much better that they removed both catheter and infusion bag. She ate solid food for breakfast. Victoria visited her at noon and then told her that she was heading home.

"You know there are armed guards outside your room?" Victoria asked.

"There are?" Erin asked.

"US Marshals, they said."

"Gosh. That's not good."

Victoria looked at her. "They do witness protection, right?"

"I'm not sure."

"I am. Dalton told me what happened out there. It's a miracle either of you is still alive. I don't know what I'd do without you."

Their embrace was tentative, but Erin survived it without too much discomfort.

"I'll see you soon," said Erin.

"I hope so. Love you." With that, her sister was gone.

Erin followed her with her eyes, stopping when she saw Dalton leaning on the doorjamb, obviously giving them time to say goodbye.

Something in his expression made her uneasy.

"What's happening, Dalton? Victoria said there are police out there."

He came in and sat in the padded orange vinyl chair beside her bed, the one she was supposed to be allowed to sit in this afternoon.

Erin offered her hand and Dalton took it in both of his.

"Are we still in danger?"

"We are. The FBI has turned us over to the US Marshals."

Her heartbeat pulsed in the swollen tissues at her neck, sending sharp stabs of pain radiating through her shoulder and arm.

"Witness protection services. Right?"

He nodded grimly.

"We have to go?"

"It's voluntary but until they know who is after us and if there are more..." His words trailed off.

"Does my sister know?"

"She saw them sitting there," said Dalton. "They frisked her."

"They did not!"

Dalton made a face that said he was not teasing.

"Have you spoken to your parents?"

"Just Helen. She's going to bring Mom up to see us."

"Your father?"

"If we decide to go, they'll bring him, too."

"What have we gotten tangled up in, Dalton?"

"Some very bad, very dangerous people who are unfortunately also well financed. Our guys don't know who is behind them yet. Have to follow the money. Large corporation or foreign government, I suppose."

"Are we going to have to leave?"

"They're recommending it."

She drew a breath and held it, studying him. "Together?" she asked.

He gripped her hand. "Erin, I know I put you in danger out there and I'm so sorry. You might not believe me, but you are the most important thing in the world to me and I hope you'll let me prove it."

"How?"

"I'm thinking I should see a counselor. See why I keep doing this."

"You think maybe that psychologist you were required to see after that deadly force thing might be right? That this has to do with your military service?"

His head dropped. "I was their platoon leader,

Erin. It was my job to look out for them. Keep them safe."

"An impossible task."

"Maybe. But I failed." He met her gaze, and his eyes glittered with grief and helplessness. "They trusted me to look out for them."

"It was a war," she reminded.

"Military action."

"With bombs and gunfire and schools used as shields."

"Yes. All that," he agreed. "I just keep feeling responsible. That I don't deserve…"

"What?" she asked.

"You. My life."

She gasped at that. In all the time since he'd left the service, he'd never said such a thing before.

She thought about all the chances he'd taken since discharge from the service. He'd only ended his military career because of her and her threats of separation. Now the pieces began to snap into place. Was he looking for a second chance to save his men? Or a second chance to die with them?

How was it that she'd never realized that his risky behavior coincided with the loss of so many of his men over in what he called the Sandbox?

"Counseling sounds smart," she said.

"A beginning place." He dragged a hand through his hair and then let his arm drop wearily back to his side. "The marshals, if we choose relocation, told me I can't be involved in law enforcement."

"All I've ever wanted was to keep you around," she said, the tears burning her throat and making her shoulder throb.

He chuckled. "Funny way of showing me that. Throwing me out, I mean."

"I tried other things first. You didn't hear me. Then after you got shot, I just couldn't stop worrying. Couldn't put it aside. It was consuming me. Eating me alive."

"I'm sorry. I don't think I understood that. I just thought you were being overly protective. That you'd get past it like all the other times. But seeing you out there, watching you get shot, well, it scared me to death."

Their eyes met and held. She knew it instantly. He understood. Finally and irrevocably, he comprehended what it was like to face the death of the person whose loss you knew you could not survive.

"I couldn't live if something happened to you, Erin. I'm sorry I didn't understand. That I didn't listen."

Tears streamed down her face as she gripped his hand. She wanted to hold him, but she could not lift her arm without hitting that morphine button and she needed a clear head.

"I just wanted you safe. It's all I ever wanted."

He gave her a sad smile. They'd come to an understanding, she thought.

"Dalton, I want to go home."

"It might be a new home."

"With the dogs?"

"The…" He laughed. "You *are* feeling better. I'll see if we can arrange that."

"Are they both all right?"

"Yes. Lulu has a new dog bed and Jet has already devoured two Frisbees."

"Where are they?"

"Your sister took them back home with her."

"I want to keep them. Lulu and Jet. Can the marshals arrange that?"

"I'll ask."

"So, the relocation…is it permanent?"

"Shouldn't be. Just until they sort out this group."

"Siming's Army."

He nodded.

She tentatively moved her arm and winced. "That will be hard, losing everyone, my family."

"It's a big decision."

Someone stood at the door and cleared his throat. They turned and Erin saw a man in green scrubs holding a clipboard. Was this the surgeon who had stopped the bleeding and saved her life?

"How are you feeling, Erin?"

She smiled at him as he approached the bed. He was handsome, with symmetrical features, of average size and above average physique. His brown hair needed a trim and the manicured stubble of a beard covered his face.

"I'm Ryan Carr," he said, and offered his hand to Dalton, who rose to shake his hand. The two released the brief clasping of palms and Carr continued around the bed, looking at her IV. She no longer had the solution dripping into her arm, but the needle remained in her vein.

"Did you say 'Carr'?" asked Dalton. Where had he heard that name before?

"How is your pain level?" asked Carr.

"I haven't used the morphine this morning."

He smiled. "That's good." He turned to Dalton and motioned to the chair. "Would you like to sit down, Detective Stevens?"

Her husband now had his hands on his hips and his brow had descended low over his dark eyes. She knew the look. Her husband sensed a threat.

Chapter Twenty-One

Dalton realized that Ryan Carr, though dressed appropriately for hospital staff, with the Crocs, scrubs and ID tag on a lanyard, gave off a totally different vibe.

Less like a healer and more like a predator.

"What did you say your position here is?" asked Dalton, not taking a seat and instead moving to stand between Carr and his wife.

"Very good, Stevens," said Carr. "You really are very good. Most people don't even notice me."

His wife spoke from behind him. "Women would notice you."

That made Dalton's frown deepen. He was attractive if you liked pretty boys.

"You need to back up out of this room," said Dalton, keeping his attention on Carr's hands, which held only the clipboard.

"I just wanted to warn you. Mind if I get my ID? My real ID?"

"I do mind. But go ahead. Slowly," said Dalton,

prepared to body slam this intruder if he even looked at Erin again. He had touched her arm, checked her IV and demonstrated very clearly how easy it was to get to them.

And then he remembered. "Ryan Carr. The chopper pilot said you gave him the cooler."

Carr nodded. "That's right."

He removed his wallet. "The marshals checked my ID, bless their hearts. But they apparently don't have a list of hospital staff. If they did," he said, taking out his identification and passing it to Dalton, "they'd know that I don't work here."

Dalton glanced at the ID with a very prominent CIA in blue on the plastic card.

"How do I know this is real or that you are who you say you are?"

"Feel free to call in and check after I go. I'm here for two reasons. First to warn you that leaving for WITSEC sooner is advisable. You are not secure here."

"And second?" asked Erin.

"To thank you. I was the one who collected that intel from a foreign operative. And I *was* the one who put it on that helicopter and gave instructions, instructions that were passed to you, Mrs. Stevens. If I understand correctly, you swam out to the pilot, attempted a rescue and took what he offered as imperative to our country's safety. Is that right?"

She nodded.

"And I'd like to thank you, Detective Stevens, for not doing as your wife requested and leaving it behind…on a red T-shirt, is that correct?" He smiled.

Dalton knew that only the FBI and CIA who had interviewed them should know these details. Was this guy for real?

"I am who I say, Detective. A fact that Agent Tillman will verify."

"We've already been lied to by someone claiming to be DHS, so excuse my skepticism."

"Lawrence Foster, yes, he proves my point—about your safety, I mean. The Justice Department is a fine organization generally. Good for moving career criminals into nice new neighborhoods after they testify. But this group, Siming's Army, they are not your typical wise guy looking to get even. They are organized and funded, backed by foreign nationals, according to my contacts. The information you rescued will be instrumental in making my case and it has already reached its terminus. The CDC is analyzing the virus and vaccine. And all because of your bravery, Mrs. Stevens." He bowed to Erin and then turned to Dalton. "And your dogged determination. Thank you both. Your country owes you a debt."

"You're welcome," said Erin.

Carr backed away from the bed and then headed for the hall, pausing to meet Dalton's troubled stare.

"Call Tillman. Tell him Carr says we need to relocate you today."

"The CIA relocates people?" asked Erin.

"We are a full-service organization, ma'am. Best of luck to you both."

He disappeared into the hall. Dalton followed him as far as the seated marshal. Carr had vanished.

"Get your boss in here now."

ERIN'S STITCHES TUGGED as she transferred to the wheelchair under heavy guard. It turned out that their visitor, Ryan Carr, was exactly who and what he claimed. The real deal, apparently. An honest-to-goodness spy who had done exactly what he claimed, rescuing the package from repeated attempts at recovery by members of Siming's Army and then finally reaching the airlift location, only to watch the chopper be shot down.

Erin thought that he must have been only ten or twelve miles from where the helicopter crashed.

But right now, Erin's main concern was to not throw up as she was wheeled down the hall under the protection of a ridiculous number of men armed with rifles. The hallway to and from the elevator was absolutely devoid of people.

"Did we just go up?" she asked Dalton.

The elevator was making her sour stomach more upset.

"Yes."

"Why?" She swallowed back the bitter taste in her mouth.

"Evac helicopter is taking us out of here."

"Like the one that Siming's Army already shot down?"

Beside her, Agent Kane Tillman leaned close. "Appreciate it if you don't mention them."

She nodded her understanding.

The next twenty minutes were a blur. She only threw up once and the attending EMTs seemed used to this sort of disturbance. They gave her something that settled her stomach and something for the pain. But the analgesic made her sleepy. Now she struggled to stay awake.

The sky was a deep blue and the lights below them flicked on. Streets glimmered with lines of red taillights and white headlights, strung in parallel ribbons.

"Where are we heading?" she asked, watching the Adirondacks resume custody of the land now stretching below in darkness. She stared out at a complete absence of lights and land broken occasionally by the soft glow of dusk gleaming on a lake or river. Her stretcher pressed against one window and her incline allowed her to see forward to the pilots and down to the emptiness between them and the wilderness. She searched for familiar landmarks and saw what could only be the Hudson River, larger now and dotted with the occasional river town. She saw the Mohawk merge and the twin bridges that told her they were headed south. What was their destination?

She did not have long to wonder.

"Are we descending?" she asked Dalton.

"Seems so."

"Dalton?"

He held her hand. "Hmm?"

"I can't stay awake."

He kissed her forehead. "I got you, Erin."

The drug was seeping into her bloodstream like tea in warm water. She blinked and forced her eyes open, but they rolled back in her head and her muscles went slack.

"No," she whispered, or merely thought she spoke. Had her lips moved? She drifted, torn loose from the mooring of pain, knowing that if danger came it would find her defenseless.

DALTON HAD A long night and now sat on the front porch as the birds began their morning songs. They had arrived at the temporary safe house on a country road in a little village in a county called Delaware. He'd never been to central New York. Their hostess was a woman who ran an orchard. Peaches were in season and the bees already droned in the honeysuckle bush that bordered the porch.

Erin was in an upstairs room with Roger Toddington, a former army paramedic and an EMT who was also their hostess's son. Somehow Dalton had dropped into a crazy world of espionage and he felt like Alice slipping through the looking glass. Everything seemed so normal here, but it was not.

The outside of this farmhouse looked typical enough, but the adjoining outbuilding was not the garage it appeared to be; instead, it was a fully equipped operating room with an adjoining recovery suite that rivaled the ICU where Erin had convalesced from her surgery.

Their hostess, Mrs. Arldine Toddington, offered him a cup of black coffee. The woman was fit, thin and muscular with hair that was snow-white on top and red and white beneath. She looked about as much like a spy as Mr. Rogers, God rest him. But according to Tillman she was a former US marine, a nurse practitioner with unique experience with gunshot wounds and was, it seemed, even tougher than she looked. She also made an amazing peach-and-walnut coffee cake.

But if Agent Tillman was to be believed, they were safe here and would remain in Mrs. Toddington's care until Erin recovered enough to travel without drawing attention to her healing bullet wound.

"Estimate that will be twelve to fifteen days," said Arldine.

"Do you have a location?" Dalton asked Tillman.

"Two, actually." Tillman set aside his coffee to accept a fork and a plate with a large piece of coffee cake littered with sticky walnut bits. "Thank you, Arldine."

"We'll have a choice?" asked Dalton.

Arldine and Tillman exchanged looks, and Arldine withdrew to lean against the porch rail facing them. Tillman nodded and she took over the conversation.

"We understand your wife has asked you for a legal separation."

Dalton lowered the plate to his lap and forced himself to swallow. The moist cake had turned chalky in his mouth, and the sticky topping made the food lodge in his throat.

Tillman filled the silence. "Safer for you both if you go separate ways. You are a big guy. Distinctive looking. Erin is more attractive than most women, but with a change of hair color and wardrobe, she can fit in just about anywhere."

Sweat popped out behind his ears and across his upper lip.

"Now you're saying that if we stay together, I put her at risk?"

"We are," said Tillman.

"But a few moments ago you said you could keep us safe."

"Carr has uncovered more information on this outfit. Seems to be heavily funded from offshore accounts, and we do not have a handle on the number of recruited members or even how many more sleeper cells can be activated. The speed of their response is daunting. They definitely have our attention."

"Erin and I are no threat."

"But you are on a kill list."

Dalton sat back in the rocker, sending it tilting at a dangerous angle. He knew what a kill list was. Crime organizations used them. It was a bounty list of sorts with a price on the heads of people who had betrayed or wronged them in some way.

"How do you know?" asked Dalton.

"We've gotten that much from Lawrence Foster. It was why Carr made his appearance. He doesn't usually get involved with civilians. But you two protected the information he had carried. So he felt a certain debt. He was at the hospital when I arrived, watching over you and your wife."

The man gave Dalton the creeps, and that was saying something when you considered all the types of criminals and military badasses he had come in contact with over the years.

"Where will you send her?" asked Dalton, getting back to the crux of the situation.

"I'm afraid I can't tell you that. Only the location we plan to send you."

Dalton would not even be allowed to know where she was.

"We will give you regular updates on her condition and will notify you both immediately when we neutralize the threat."

Neutralized, he thought. Also known as dead, killed, KIA or otherwise squashed.

"I need to talk this over with Erin."

"Of course," said Arldine. "You should."

"But remember that the threat increases if you stay together."

Chapter Twenty-Two

Dalton dreaded this conversation. He had come up here to win back his wife and save their marriage. Now he was going to blow it up again. Only this time he had a good reason. He was doing it to save Erin. To protect her, he had to leave her.

Impossible. Necessary.

He rubbed a knuckle back and forth across his wrinkled forehead trying to prepare for the conversation. She was just recovering, only off the morphine for one day, but he did not have time to waste. The longer he waited, the higher the chances that he would back out. Thinking of the look on her face and of never seeing that face again might just be enough to kill him. According to her, he'd been trying to do that—kill himself—ever since he came home from the Sandbox. He realized she had been right all along and so he would see a mental health professional ASAP. Or he could throw himself right back into the action. He could decline relocation and reenlist.

He felt as if his stomach was filled with tiny

shards of glass, cutting him apart from the inside. He stood before her door, an upstairs bedroom of Arldine's farmhouse with southern exposure, lots of light and a fine view of the hayfield across the road.

Dalton rapped on the door. Roger called him in. When Dalton did not enter, the EMT appeared at the door, his face fixed with a gentle smile.

"Come on in, Detective. I'm just finishing." Roger looped his stethoscope around his neck and held the ends as one might do with a small towel.

Dalton stepped in on wooden legs. Would she believe him? He had to make her believe him.

"Hey there," Erin said.

She sat up in the hospital-style bed, a bouquet of sunflowers in a blue ceramic pitcher beside her on the bedside table. Beneath them rested a pill bottle, a half-empty water glass and a magazine.

"How are you feeling?"

"Lonely. I asked Roger to let me move back with you. I understand you have a queen mattress and a view of the barn."

He hadn't noticed the view, except that there was easy access to a flat roof beneath the window and a short drop to the ground from there.

The thick bandage on her neck was all the incentive he needed to do what he must. Dalton drew up the old wooden chair and placed it backward beside her bed. He sat, straddling the chair back, using the dowels as a sort of barrier between them because he feared that if he touched her, he'd never let her go.

Dalton cleared his throat.

"Honey?" asked Erin. "What's wrong?"

ERIN FELT THE worry creeping up her spine like a nest of baby spiders, their tiny legs moving over her back, lifting the hairs on her body and washing her skin cold.

Dalton's expression was unfamiliar and deadly serious.

She hazarded a guess.

"Are they out there?" She motioned toward the window and winced, forgetting not to use her left hand. Her head was clear thanks to ceasing the narcotics, but the pain pulsed with her heart, and her healing skin and muscle burned with the slightest movement.

"No, they're not. Erin, we are going to different locations."

"What?" Confusion mingled with the fear, landing in her stomach and squeezing tight. She sat up, leaving her nest of pillows, ignoring the pain that now bloomed across her chest. "No."

"It's what you wanted. A separation."

"Trial separation and I explained that to you. I don't want a separation. I want you to stop taking unnecessary risks. To see a counselor as you said."

"I changed my mind."

Her mouth dropped open. She could not even formulate a reply.

"I'm not leaving the force."

"But…wait…no…" She was stammering. "You

have to leave the force. We're relocating. You can't…
Dalton, this makes no sense."

"You said I have a death wish. I'm agreeing with
you."

"This is suicide."

He nodded.

"You have to come with me."

"I'm not."

"What are you doing, Dalton? Are they using you
as some kind of bait again? We got them Foster. They
cannot expect you—"

"They don't. Haven't. I just thought you deserved
to hear it from me. I'm leaving *you* this time. I'm
sorry, Erin. People don't change. Sooner or later,
I'm catching a bullet. I'm ready. Ready to join those
guys I promised to protect."

"Oh no, you don't." She reached for him.

He stood, looking down at her with regret. But not
love. Somehow that was gone. The coldness in his
dark eyes momentarily stopped her breathing, and
her hand dropped to the bright pastel quilt.

"Goodbye, Erin."

The pain solidified like the surface of a frozen
lake. She pointed a finger at him.

"Dalton, don't you dare walk out that door!"

But he was already gone, and the door slammed
shut behind him.

DALTON MADE IT only to the top of the stairs. Tillman
stood on the landing a few steps below him. Dalton
sank to the top step still gripping the banister.

"She believe you?"

He nodded, thinking he did not have the strength to rise.

"Good. You can leave now. I have your location information."

"Where?"

Chapter Twenty-Three

Erin adjusted the wide-brimmed ranger hat on her head and proceeded toward her truck, the radio clunking against her hip with each stride. She paused to pass out a few stickers to the children in a visiting family who had stopped to read the nature trail board at the start of a gentle two-mile hike.

"Thank you!" piped the middle child. The youngest was already trying unsuccessfully to affix the sticker on her shirt without removing the backing and the eldest squatted in front of her to help.

Erin waved, feeling just the slightest tug in the stiff muscles of her neck. The cold in the mountains seemed to creep into the place where she had been shot.

She crossed the lot to her truck. Her new location was Mount Rainer National Park where she spent more time outside than she had on the East Coast. Unfortunately, she did not teach rock climbing or lead nature hikes for groups visiting from all over the world. That would be too much like her old life. So she did patrols, taught classes to youngsters in the nature center and manned the admission booth. At night she presented educational programs in the outdoor amphitheater for the visitors camping on-site.

Once in her truck, she unzipped her heavy jacket and headed back to the station past the yellow aspen and spectacular views of the ridge of blue mountains. She lived close to the station in the housing provided by the park to the rangers. Lulu and Jet greeted her at the door, as always. She had spent many nights alone back in Yonkers while Dalton worked his cases. And, though she had worried, she'd known he was out there and hoped he would be home eventually. Now that hope was gone. The cabin had a hollow feel and if not for the dogs, she didn't think she could take the solitude. Even with the other rangers she was alone, sticking to the story they had given her that made her five years younger and an only child.

September in New York was cool and lovely, but here in the Cascades the high altitude changed the seasons early. There was already snow predicted in the Cascades. In downstate New York, the earliest she ever saw snow had been November, and often just flurries, but here it was September 7 and predictions were for an accumulation tomorrow.

She didn't mind, could not have asked for a more perfect relocation. And the Company, as they self-identified, were optimistic that she would not have to stay here for more than a year. The information she and Dalton had furnished was likely to stop a pandemic.

Agent Carr kept in touch, appearing erratically to join a hike or as a solo camper applying for a wilderness permit. He said they were in the process of finding the three Deathbringers that were mentioned on the thumb drive.

The three Deathbringers, according to Carr, came from Chinese folklore, though even in myth form they were still considered dangerous by many. These "corpses" were believed by some to enter the body just after birth and determined the life span of each individual. Each corpse attacked a different system, brain, heart and organs. More specifically to the CIA, they would attack US citizens. The virus that she and Dalton had carried attacked the internal organs, causing a massive shutdown of the renal system. That was corpse number one and steps were underway to locate and intercept a shipment of this virus before it reached US soil. The second corpse, which attacked the brain, referred to a cyber attack, already in place, the brain being a metaphor for the infrastructure that kept communication open. Their people were working on that one now, as well. And the heart? Carr said that the Company believed this was an airborne toxin in production somewhere in New York State.

At the cabin she glimpsed a rental car. A man stood on the porch beside Jet, and for just a moment her heart galloped. But then she recognized that the stranger was too small to be Dalton.

She didn't look over her shoulder or jump every time she heard an unfamiliar sound. She just was not living her life like that. Erin was out of the vehicle and greeting Jet before she recognized the man in the cowboy hat.

"Mr. Carr," she said. "That hat makes you look like a Texas Ranger."

He slipped down the stairs to shake her hand. "A pleasure to see you again."

He smiled. "And you."

"Staying for supper?" she asked.

"No, unfortunately. Just wanted to tell you that the tech team has located the computer virus their hackers installed. It was set to disrupt two different systems. The rails in NYC, including subways, and the gas and electric grid in Buffalo."

"Can they stop it?"

"Working on that now."

She finished stroking Jet's head and the canine moved off to explore around the cabin. Erin hoped the porcupine she'd seen last night was now sleeping in a tree somewhere.

Lulu barked from inside. Erin let her out and Carr in.

"Can I fix you some coffee?"

He nodded.

She didn't ask if he'd like a beer, knowing he always turned her down.

"We are working to shut down the cell that came after you. Early indications are that they did not pass on any information about you or Dalton."

"What does that mean, exactly?"

"If we can ascertain that no other cell of the terrorist organization is aware of your involvement, it would mean you could return to your family."

It took only a moment for the coffee to brew. She used the time to force down the lump in her throat. To be able to return to her life would be wonderful, but one member of her family was absent. She missed Dalton so much her body ached from the sorrow. Erin forced her shoulders back and she passed Carr a mug of black coffee.

"Erin?" he asked, his face showing concern as he accepted the mug.

"That's good news." She managed the words, but her voice quavered. "How are my parents?"

"Missing you. But fine."

"My sister?"

"Said to tell you that the middle one lost a front tooth."

Erin smiled. "That's Patrick. I hope he didn't knock it out." He was in second grade, and all his classmates had that same gap-toothed smile and whistling disability.

She never asked about Dalton out of a mixture of sorrow and fear. They would tell her if and when he was killed. Wouldn't they?

The panic that they wouldn't forced her to tip heavily against the kitchen counter. Summoning her courage, she fixed her gaze on Carr.

"What's the word on Dalton? Is he still with the New York City Real Time Crime Center?"

The mug in Carr's hand paused at his lip and he regarded her a moment in silence. Then he lowered the mug to the counter.

"What was that?"

"I'm asking if he's back with his unit?"

"Erin, we told Dalton that joint relocation was dangerous because Dalton is so…" He extended his arms, indicating Dalton's unusual size. Carr's hand then went up to indicate Dalton's above-average height. "So…distinctive. You both agreed to separate locations."

"I'm confused," she said. "Dalton turned down relocation."

Carr arched a single brow that told her instantly that she had something wrong.

"Yes. I was aware he told you that," said Carr.

"Turned it down," she said, trying to convince Carr as the panic constricted her throat. "He told me that he couldn't change and that he would miss the action, the danger. He told me…" She made a fist and scrubbed it across her forehead. "He said…" She lifted her gaze to Carr. "He relocated?"

"He was. He just didn't tell you."

Her knees went out and she sank down along the lower cabinets, stopping only when her backside hit the floor.

"He lied to me."

Carr was beside her in an instant, squatting before her. "You signed the papers agreeing to separate locations."

She glared up at him. "Clearly, I didn't read the fine print."

"That was unwise."

She rested her forehead on her folded forearms supported by her knees. She spoke to her lap. "I would never have agreed…"

And that was why Dalton had not told her.

"Exactly," said Carr his expression showing regret.

She concentrated on breathing through her nose until the dark moth-like spots flapped away from her vision. Then she lifted her head.

"Why tell me now?" she asked.

"It seemed wrong to me. And you are unhappy."

"I want to see him."

"Marshalls service will tell you that is impossible."

"Really?" she said. "Then I'm taking out an ad in the *Seattle Times*."

"That will get you killed."

"Want to stop me? Take me to Dalton."

"I can't do that."

She was up and snatching the keys from the bowl beside the door. Jet trotted after her. Lulu came at a waddle.

Outside she opened the truck door and Jet jumped in. Lulu needed a boost. She was behind the wheel when Carr reached her, on the phone, talking fast to someone and then to her. "Where are you going, Erin?"

"Yonkers."

He stood in the open door, keeping her from closing it.

"I could arrest you as a threat to national security."

"You told me what happened. Now you can take me to Dalton."

"He did this to protect you. If you leave WITSEC, his sacrifice is for nothing."

"The heck with that. I only agreed to this arrangement because he lied to me."

"Which is why he did this."

"I'll sue."

"You can't sue us."

Erin turned the key in the ignition. Carr reached in and flicked the engine back off.

"You knew what I'd do when I found out."

Carr shrugged. "Surmised."

He was playing her. Why did he want her to break cover?

"Why?" she asked.

"He's unhappy, too. Seems poor payment for your service."

"Take me to him," she whispered.

"All right," said Carr.

Chapter Twenty-Four

Dalton returned from his monthlong job on an offshore oil rig in the Gulf of Mexico on calm waters. The transport vessel slowed to dock in Mobile, Alabama. The replacement crew was behind them, and he and his new coworker were off for four glorious weeks. The gulf was the color of the Caribbean Sea today as they reached shallow water, and the sky was a pale summer blue. Though fall had taken firm hold up north, here the summer stretched long and warm.

He let the young ones hurry off the vessel first— those with girlfriends and new wives who still cared enough to greet them upon disembarking. The older men and the single ones had no one waiting and could make their way leisurely to their trucks and Harleys to head to wherever they went when not working thirteen-hour shifts. Dalton wondered where Erin was today. Was she looking at a blue sky or gray clouds? Was it raining where she was? Was she safe? Did she miss him?

"See you soon, Carl," said one of the roustabouts he had come to know.

He touched two fingers to his forehead, tanned from all the outdoor work, and gave a sloppy salute.

His roommate, a motorman from the Florida Panhandle, slapped him on the back as he headed down the gangplank, which led to the receiving area where family sometimes waited.

"Bye, Carl."

"Safe drive, Randall," he called after him.

His position as an offshore installation manager was made easier by the real manager who was teaching him the job. Dalton's own experiences working on so many task forces definitely made the transition easier. And he was used to getting off duty only to be called back up the instant he fell asleep because that part of the job was exactly the same.

But he'd always had Erin to come home to.

He adjusted his duffel bag on his shoulder and exited the gangway over the pier and headed into the arrival facility. His body had healed, leaving only the entrance and exit wound from the bullet that had broken his marriage.

"Wasn't the bullet. It was you."

Had Erin's wound healed?

He crossed the lobby, passing the couples reunited after their offshore stints. He was surprised to see so many children here on a school day, greeting dads.

Nice, he thought.

The bureau had furnished him with a three-year-old red pickup truck and he headed to the lot, hoping it would start after sitting in the blazing sun for a month.

Dalton cleared the lobby of the company's dockside offices and was hit by the heat and humidity. Without the boat's motion, the breeze had ceased and he began to sweat. He hurried down the sidewalk toward the lot, anxious to reach the air-conditioning of his truck.

But where was he going? Back to his empty condo? Not likely. He'd have a meal first. One where he could pick what he wanted from a menu. And a beer. He'd missed having a cold one on a hot day.

He caught motion in his peripheral vision, his brain relaying that there was an animal running toward him. He turned to give a knee to any dog stupid enough to jump on him. Dalton dropped his duffel as his hand went automatically to his hip to find no service weapon waiting.

The dog was black, a skinny Lab with a new pink collar. The dog seemed familiar and wagged frantically as Dalton stared in confusion. It whined and bowed and fell to its back kicking all four feet.

That almost looked like…impossible.

This dog could not be that dog. But then, waddling around between a pigmy palm and a hydrangea bush awash in hot-pink blooms, came a fat pug dog.

"Lulu?" he asked. He turned back to the black dog as he dropped to one knee. "Jet?"

Jet's reply was a sharp bark. Then she threw herself into Dalton's arms, wriggling and lapping his face with her long, wet tongue.

Dalton scooped up Lulu and stared at her. The dog seemed to smile and panted as if the walk had been taxing. Dalton returned her to the ground and she dropped to one hip as he shot to his feet.

Erin. She had to be here. But that was impossible.

Dalton scanned his surroundings, fixing on the only running vehicle that had dark tinted glass.

He turned to see a woman stepping from the rear seat of a large, dark SUV, the sort you might see in a presidential motorcade. Sunglasses hid her eyes and her hair was shorter, darker and much more stylish. Her mouth lifted in a familiar smile. Was she wearing red lipstick?

"Hey, sailor," she said.

She slammed the door shut, giving him a view of the flowery, sheer halter top and short cutoff jeans. The pale skin told him that wherever she had been it was cold, for it looked as if she had not seen the sun since he last saw her.

Jet darted back to her and then reeled and dashed back to Dalton. Lulu sat looking at her mistress, content to wait for her to catch up.

From the opposite side of the SUV stepped CIA agent Ryan Carr. "I got a delivery for you," he said, tipping a thumb toward Erin.

"Where do I sign?" asked Dalton.

"We have an escort in the lot. They'll take you to your new location."

"Where?"

"New Mexico. Tourist town outside Sedona."

Erin lowered her glasses and studied him, taking a moment, it seemed, to absorb the changes. If he'd known he would have cut his hair, shaved his face. He rasped his knuckles over the stubble that was well on its way to becoming a beard.

He blinked at her, trying to understand and then taking two steps in her direction before the truth struck him.

They were blown.

Dalton turned to Carr.

"When?" he asked as he strode toward Erin. He needed her back in the car. Out of sight. What was the agent doing letting her be seen out here?

"When, what?"

"We're blown," he said.

Carr shook his head. "You're not. Just a change of plans."

Erin reached him now, slipped her arms around his middle and pressed herself to him. He gathered her up in his arms and lowered his head, inhaling the familiar scent as he took in the changes. She was thinner.

He drew back to look at her, seeing the puckering red scar at the juncture of her shoulder and neck. A shot through the muscle that had torn into a major blood vessel and nearly taken her life.

Erin flipped her sunglasses up to her head and stared up at him. The look was not longing or desperate unrequited love. It seemed more like a smoldering fury that he had seen too many times in their marriage.

She lowered her chin. "You said you wanted a separation."

"I said that."

"You never told me the reason. So what is it, exactly?"

He pressed his mouth shut, not wanting to spoil this. To see her again, it was too sweet, and even having her mad was having her.

"Dalton?" Her arms slipped from his waist and folded before her. One slim sandaled foot began tapping the hot sidewalk.

"They said you'd be safer away from me. That I stand out."

She threw up her hands. Then she slugged him in the chest. He absorbed the blow. He knew from experience that she had a better right than that. This was just a mark of displeasure.

"You were protecting me?"

He nodded.

"You still love me?"

He nodded again.

"Then get in the car." She motioned to the SUV.

"Yes, dear." Dalton slipped into the rear seat. Erin retrieved Lulu, who had collapsed to her side, and then snapped her fingers for Jet, who bounded onto the rear seat and sprawled across Dalton's lap.

Then Erin climbed in and closed the door, ordering the dogs off the seat.

In the front area Carr was already buckling into the driver's seat and put them in Reverse.

Erin touched a button on the armrest and the privacy window lifted. Once it had closed completely, she tossed aside her glasses and grasped his face between her two small hands. Then she gave him the sort of kiss that had his eyes closing to absorb the perfection of the contact.

When she drew back, they sat side by side, breathless, hearts racing. She curled her hands around one of his arms and lowered her head to his shoulder.

"I missed you every minute. I can't believe you'd do this without telling me."

"Would you have gone?"

She shook her head. "I love you, Dalton. And marrying you was my way of letting you know that I wanted to spend the rest of my life *with* you."

He closed his eyes as he wondered if being apart, safe and miserable was preferable to accepting the increased risk and being with his wife. Then he decided it was not.

"I was wrong," he said. "I know it. I knew it almost immediately after I left you, but it was too late."

"Apparently not."

"How did you get them to come for me?"

"Threatened to walk away, tell the papers all about it."

He sat back, stunned. "You can't do that. You signed an agreement."

She shrugged.

"You threatened the CIA?"

Erin's cheeks turned pink. "I did."

"They make people disappear for that."

"We're small fish. Best to just let us go."

"I'm glad you did," he admitted. "So glad. I've been miserable without you, Erin. You're more than a piece of me—you're my heart."

She hugged him. "Oh, Dalton."

They drove in silence behind the escort car and trailed by another, winding through the streets and toward the highway.

"Where are they taking us now?" he asked.

"Airport first. And then, who cares? As long as we are together."

He gathered her up in his arms, dragging her to his lap for another kiss. She was right again. It didn't matter where they went. It mattered only that she had never stopped loving him and that he had her back in his arms once more.

* * * * *

INTRIGUE

Available August 20, 2019

#1875 TANGLED THREAT
by Heather Graham

Years ago, FBI agent Brock McGovern was arrested for a crime he didn't commit. Now that he's been cleared of all charges, he'll do whatever it takes to find the culprit. With two women missing, Brock's ex-girlfriend Maura Antrium is eager to help him. Can they find the killer...or will he find them first?

#1876 FULL FORCE
Declan's Defenders • by Elle James

After working at the Russian embassy in Washington, DC, Emily Chastain is targeted by a relentless killer. When she calls upon Declan's Defenders in order to find someone to help her, former Force Recon marine Frank "Mustang" Ford vows to find the person who is threatening her.

#1877 THE SAFEST LIES
A Winchester, Tennessee Thriller • by Debra Webb

Special Agent Sadie Buchanen is deep in the backcountry of Winchester, Tennessee, in order to retrieve a hostage taken by a group of extreme survivalists. When she finds herself in danger, she must rely on Smith Flynn, an intriguing stranger who is secretly an undercover ATF special agent.

#1878 MURDERED IN CONARD COUNTY
Conard County: The Next Generation • by Rachel Lee

When a man is killed, Blaire Afton and Gus Maddox, two park rangers, must team up to find the murderer. Suddenly, they discover they are after a serial killer... But can they stop him before he claims another victim?

#1879 CONSTANT RISK
The Risk Series: A Bree and Tanner Thriller • by Janie Crouch

A serial killer is loose in Dallas, and only Bree Daniels and Tanner Dempsey can stop him. With bodies piling up around them, can they find the murderer before more women die?

#1880 WANTED BY THE MARSHAL
American Armor • by Ryshia Kennie

After nurse Kiera Connell is abducted by a serial killer and barely escapes with her life, she must rely on US marshal Travis Johnson's protection. But while Travis believes the murderer is in jail, Kiera knows a second criminal is on the loose and eager to silence her.

———

Get 4 FREE REWARDS!

We'll send you 2 FREE Books plus 2 FREE Mystery Gifts.

Harlequin Intrigue® books feature heroes and heroines that confront and survive danger while finding themselves irresistibly drawn to one another.

FREE
Value Over
$20

"I've been assigned to go back to Florida. To stay at the
Frampton Ranch and Resort—and investigate what we
believe to be three kidnappings and a murder. And the
kidnappings may have nothing to do with the resort,
nor may the murder?" Brock McGovern asked, a small
note of incredulity slipping into his voice, which was
surprising to him—he was always careful to keep an
even tone.

FBI assistant director Richard Egan had brought him
into his office, and Brock had known he was going on
assignment—he just hadn't expected this.

"Yes, not what you'd want, but, hey, maybe it'll be
good for you—and perhaps necessary now, when time
is of the essence and there is no one out there who could
know the place or the circumstances with the same scope

and experience you have," Egan told him. "Three young women have disappeared from the area. Two of them were guests of the Frampton Ranch and Resort shortly before their disappearances—the third had left St. Augustine and was on her way there. The Florida Department of Law Enforcement has naturally been there already. They asked for federal help on this. Shades of the past haunt them—they don't want any more unsolved murders—and everyone is hoping against hope that Lily Sylvester, Amy Bonham and Lydia Merkel might be found."

"These are Florida missing-person cases," Brock said. "And it's sad but true that young people go to Florida and get caught up in the beach life and the club scene. And regrettable but true once again—there's a drug and alcohol culture that does exist and people get caught up in it. Not just in Florida, of course, but everywhere." He smiled grimly. "I go where I'm told, but I'm curious—how is this an FBI affair? And forgive me, but—FBI out of New York?"

"Not out of New York. FDLE asked for you. Specifically."

Don't miss
Tangled Threat *by Heather Graham,*
available September 2019 wherever
Harlequin® books and ebooks are sold.

www.Harlequin.com

Need an adrenaline rush from nail-biting tales
(and irresistible males)?

Check out **Harlequin Intrigue®**,
Harlequin® Romantic Suspense and
Love Inspired® Suspense books!

New books available every month!

CONNECT WITH US AT:

Facebook.com/groups/HarlequinConnection

Facebook.com/HarlequinBooks

Twitter.com/HarlequinBooks

Instagram.com/HarlequinBooks

Pinterest.com/HarlequinBooks

ReaderService.com

**ROMANCE WHEN
YOU NEED IT**

SGENRE2018R

SPECIAL EXCERPT FROM

HQN™

Read on for a sneak preview of
Just His Luck *by B.J. Daniels.*

Another scream rose in her throat as the icy water rushed in around her. She fought to free herself, but the ropes that bound her wrists to the steering wheel held tight, chafing her skin until it tore and bled. Her throat was raw from screaming, while outside the car, the wind kicked up whitecaps on the pond. The waves lapped at the windows. Inside the car, water rose around her feet, before climbing up her legs to lap at her waist.

She pleaded for help as the water began to rise up to her chest. But anyone who might have helped her was back at the high school graduation party she'd just left. If only she'd stayed at the party. If only she hadn't burned so many bridges earlier tonight. If only…

As the water lapped against her throat, she screamed even though she knew no one was coming to her rescue. Certainly not the person standing on the shore watching.

The pond was outside of town, away from everything. She knew now that was why her killer had chosen it. Worse, no one would be looking for her, not after the way she'd behaved when she'd left the party.

"You're big on torturing people," her killer had said. "Not so much fun when the shoe is on the other foot, huh?"

More than half-drunk, the bitter taste of betrayal in her mouth, she'd wanted to beg for her life. But her pride wouldn't let her. As her hands were bound to the steering wheel, she tried to convince herself that the only reason this was happening was to scare her. No one would actually kill her. Not even someone she'd bullied at school.

She was Ariel Matheson. Everyone wanted to be her friend. Everyone wanted to be her, sexy spoiled rich girl. No one hated her enough to go through with this. Even when the car had been pushed into the pond, she told herself that her new baby blue SUV wouldn't sink. Or if it did, the water wouldn't be deep enough that she'd drown.

The dank water splashed into her face. Frantic, she tried to sit up higher, but the seat belt and the rope on her wrists held her down. The car lurched under her as it wallowed almost full of water on the rough surface of the pond. Waves washed over the windshield, obscuring the lights of Whitefish, Montana, as the SUV slowly began to sink and she felt the last few minutes of her life slipping away.

She spit out a mouthful and told herself that this wasn't happening. Things like this didn't happen to her. This was not the way her life would end. It couldn't be.

Panic made her suck in another mouthful of awful-tasting water. She tried to hold her breath as she told herself that she was destined for so much more. The girl most likely to end up with everything she wanted, it said in her yearbook.

Bubbles rose around her as the car filled to the headliner, forcing her to let out the breath she'd been holding. This was real. This wasn't just to scare her.

The last thing she saw before the SUV sank the rest of the way was her killer standing on the bank in the dark night, watching her die. Would anyone miss her? Mourn her? She'd made so many enemies. Would anyone even come looking for her in the days ahead? Her parents would think that she'd run away. Her friends…

Fury replaced her fear. They thought she was a bitch before? As water filled her lungs, she swore that if she had it to do over, she'd make them all pay.

Don't miss
Just His Luck *by B.J. Daniels,*
available September 2019 wherever
Harlequin® books and ebooks are sold.

www.Harlequin.com

Love Harlequin romance?

DISCOVER.

Be the first to find out about promotions, news and exclusive content!

f Facebook.com/HarlequinBooks

🐦 Twitter.com/HarlequinBooks

📷 Instagram.com/HarlequinBooks

P Pinterest.com/HarlequinBooks

ReaderService.com

EXPLORE.

Sign up for the Harlequin e-newsletter and download a free book from any series at **TryHarlequin.com.**

CONNECT.

Join our Harlequin community to share your thoughts and connect with other romance readers!
Facebook.com/groups/HarlequinConnection

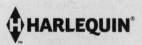

HARLEQUIN®

**ROMANCE WHEN
YOU NEED IT**

HSOCIAL2018